Hotwife Hotel Adultery - A Naughty Romance Hot Wife Novel

Karly Violet

Published by Karly Violet, 2020.

Hotwife Hotel Adultery
A Naughty Romance Hot Wife Novel

Author's note: All character in this story are 18 years of age and older. This is a work of fiction, any resemblance to real live name or events are purely coincidental.

Be aware: This story is written for, and should only be enjoyed by, ADULTS. It includes explicit descriptions of intense sexual activity between consenting adults.

Note that this work of fiction resembles a fantasy world, all events taking place are a result of a role play amongst all parties and all parties are fully consenting adults.

This is a work of fiction. Similarities to real people, places, or events are entirely coincidental.

HOTWIFE HOTEL ADULTERY - A NAUGHTY ROMANCE HOT WIFE NOVEL

First edition. December 2, 2020.

ISBN: 979-8201281762

Written by Karly Violet.

Sign up to my Patreon account and receive exclusive Hotwife stories every month and sexy scenes every week!

https://www.patreon.com/karlyviolet

Chapter One: A Hard Confession

I love my wife. Everything about her, from her strikingly dark brown eyes and shoulder length hair of the same color, to her athletic body and sharp mind, makes me swoon a bit when I think about her. For ten years we have been married and have lived in Brighton Falls. For all those years I have owned a local furniture store that I inherited from my parents. Things have gone well enough, I suppose, but there are times when sales are down and tensions in our house run high. Still, my beautiful wife and I have persevered through thick and thin, until today. Today causes me to wonder what our future will be like if things are as bad as my wife says they are.

"I'm sorry," Tori tells me as she begins to cry, dabbing her eyes with a small handkerchief. "I didn't mean for everything to go like this, Andy."

Shaking my head, I look down at my hands and think for a moment before asking, "What the hell were you thinking when you did it, Tori? You were put into that position because you were highly respected, but now you tell me that the trust the council put in you was misplaced?"

"I'm so sorry, honey." My wife takes my hand as she cries, tears now streaming down her face. Tori is afraid of what is to come now that she has been informed by the prosecuting attorney's office that there is an investigation into allegations that she has embezzled money from the city government's coffers. At first, as Tori was telling me this a few minutes ago, I thought that she was joking with me. However, it took very little time before I began to realize that she is honestly scared for her life. It's hard to understand why Tori would do such a thing, though.

"Why are you telling me this?" I ask as I look over at her. "Shouldn't you keep your mouth shut about whether you have been doing something illegal? What if they question me?"

"You can't be made to testify against me, Andy. Since we are married, there is some legal protection there."

"Okay," I reply. "But you are still taking a huge risk. They can't *compel* me to give evidence, but I could offer it. Why do you trust me with this?"

The surprise on Tori's face causes me to regret asking such a question. "I guess that if you are against me now, then it's all over anyway." My wife suddenly drops my hand and stands to her feet, walking over to the other side of the small office at the back of the furniture store.

"No, please don't misunderstand, sweetheart," I say as I jump to my feet as well. I go to where Tori is standing and put an arm around her shoulders. "That came out all wrong. You know I will not say anything to the prosecutor or anyone else."

She turns and looks back into my eyes. "I'm screwed anyway, Andy. That woman is determined, and I think she has it out for me and anyone else she can take down who works in city hall." Tori may have a point. Patricia Wood is the newly elected prosecuting attorney for our county who ran on a platform of cleaning up all the county government as well as the cities found within the county. Fate has it that Ms. Wood has begun with our little town before any other, so naturally the first place to look is in the financial records in my wife's office. As city treasurer, Tori holds record of every transaction that has taken place in Brighton Falls over the last few years, and apparently there are enough discrepancies to cause a further investigation by the young prosecuting attorney.

"I can talk to Craig to see what can be done."

"Craig?" My wife's face contorts as she thinks about the man who won the mayoral election just two years ago. "He's not the sort of guy who would put his neck on the line for anyone, Andy. The guy is slimy at best."

"He gets away with things," I tell her. "He knows how to get through most kinds of tough issues and comes out in the end smelling better than before. You know he is skimming off the top of the budget, honey." Everyone who has anything to do with city hall knows this to be the case. Craig Leighton started out as one of the crookedest used car salesmen our town has ever seen, and made a lot of money while doing it. Even though everyone sees him as being the guy who would rob his own destitute mother, everyone also goes to him to buy a car when they need one. Somehow, he has been able to convince each and every customer of his that although Craig might be a bit dishonest with some customers, he would never be dishonest with *them.* The slickest man in town became everybody's best friend even though he was fleecing them for hundreds or even thousands of dollars when they bought a used car from him. Of course he was destined to become mayor. There was no one else in town when he ran for the position who could boast of being as crooked as Craig Leighton.

"I don't even like being *around* him. He calls me *sweetie* and *honey* all the time, Andy."

"He calls every woman he knows those kinds of names, my love. Even his own sister is called *sweetie* by the guy."

"Don't involve him," Tori pleads as she takes my hand. "He can't help me anyway. All he could possibly do is make things a lot worse, honey. Besides, Craig is going to want to try to insulate himself from this whole thing, and helping me would not help that effort."

"You don't give the guy enough credit. He knows how to work people, Tori. He can talk to this new prosecutor and get her to either back off or to come to some sort of mutual arrangement."

"You mean *pay her off*." My wife's eyes look sharply up at me before she walks past me back to my desk.

"I never said that."

"Nobody ever does," she replies as she crosses her arms. "This is how I got myself into this shit in the first place. First, one guy needed a favor and then another. Next thing I knew, I was putting my own hand into the accounts to help cover some of our bills. Now I'm in so much hot water that I don't know what to do." My wife turns to look at me defiantly. "Craig Leighton is a cancerous asshole, Andy. Do *not* bring him into this."

Anger getting the best of me, I pick up a file folder from my desk and slam it back down hard, the thud almost deafening as I look back at my wife. "*You* have brought me into this, Tori. You no longer have any right to dictate to me who *can* or who *cannot* know about this mess. You also have lost the right to tell me who I can ask to help us with this. If you had kept your fingers out of the cookie jar, you wouldn't have to worry so much right now about a probe into the city's finances."

"My *fingers* in the cookie jar?" Tori slowly holds up her hand and pushes one finger above all the others, effectively offering me a vulgar response. "How is *that* for a finger?"

Turning to storm out of the office, my wife almost doesn't stop as I call out after her, "They will put you in jail, Tori." She stops but doesn't turn around. "All because you wanted money that didn't belong to you. All because you did favors for people who then turned around and did favors for you. All because you got too damned greedy."

Tori turns around and closes the office door before walking back over to me. "How do you think the electricity bill and the water bill got paid last month? With *my* paycheck? With *your* shitty sales month? No, my love, they were paid because there is a slush fund in the city account. One that I thought was very well hidden by the accounting tricks that I have learned over the past five years as treasurer. She found it. A prosecuting attorney with almost no experience as a prosecuting attorney before being elected last fall found a very small accounting trick without actually coming to my office to see the books. How do you suppose she managed that, Andy?"

I shrug my shoulders. "You tell me."

My wife's dark eyes seem to penetrate my soul as she shakes her head and replies, "Someone in city hall knows about the accounts and decided to tip her off. There is no way she could have found that without being told where it was. It's not as if I have been moving thousands of dollars every month, so I'm not being greedy, Andy. We are talking about an occasional three or four hundred dollars here and there. Maybe a total of five thousand dollars over the last five years, and only when we have needed it so badly that I dared to risk going to jail over it." Tori turns and looks out the window of my office toward the furniture sitting in the store. "You haven't sold but one or two pieces of furniture the whole fucking week, but you lecture *me?"*

"Honey, I'm not placing all of the blame on you. I know I don't earn enough sometimes and that I have put a lot of the bills off onto you. No matter what, though, you can't go and break the law without some expectation that they will catch you eventually. This prosecuting attorney is not going to stop until she has you ensnared in her net unless we get people involved who know how to deal with corruption. Craig knows better than anyone else here what to do. He knows *judges,* Tori!" I put my hands into the air before dropping them right back to my sides. "You need to stop pretending that somehow you are cleaner than the mayor and own up to what has to be done to make it through this. You need to accept any help the man is willing to give us."

My wife opens the office door again and looks out into the store. "If you call him, there's no going back, Andy. You know that he will consider us indebted to him. That's his nature, after all."

"I know."

"Craig will *never* let this go. He will hold this over our heads for as long as we live in Brighton Falls. There are a lot of people here who owe him because of what he has done for them behind the curtain. We will end up regretting his involvement, I can promise you that."

"I can handle the mayor," I reply sullenly. "I have always had a knack with him, Tori. He knows my family very well and there is a respect there that I can bank on. Craig can be trusted."

"I hope you are right." With that, my wife walks through the door and closes it behind her. Tori walks briskly through the furniture store and out the front door as I watch her leave, the only person to come into the store today.

"Dammit," I groan as I put a hand on my face. "I did not need this today." I walk over to my desk and have a seat in the old leather office chair. Picking up the phone, I try to think of what to say. Craig and I have not spoke in quite some time, although we were at one time very good friends while in high school. We both played football on the same team, winning the state championship our senior year just as our lives seemed to be getting started. Since then, we have taken very different paths in our lives. He earned a degree in marketing after high school and I was given this store from my father when he died. Though Craig can go and make whatever he wants to out of himself, I am stuck here in this town because of the furniture store. This place needs to survive, whatever I have to do to help that survival along. It is why I am resolute in calling the mayor of our small town, even over the objections of my concerned wife.

"Hey, Craig," I say into the phone as he answers on the other end. "This is Andy Dixon."

"Well, hey there!" he says to me with a bit more excitement than I expected. "I haven't heard from you in a while."

"No, I guess we have both been really busy." I rub my eyes with a hand as I ask, "Can we have a quick conversation right now?"

There is a brief pause on the phone before he replies, "Sure. What's up?"

"Tori," I say immediately.

"Oh." I can tell by the way he says it that the mayor is already very aware of the situation involving my wife.

"She's nervous, Craig. *Very* nervous."

"I can see why. Look, I don't have anything to do with the books, but I am sure you already know that. The city council, though, will have to take up this matter soon."

"I figured they would. Anyway, we need your help." I cringe as I say it, knowing that this is going to cost my wife and I a lot in some way later. My wife was correct about my old schoolmate. Craig will expect some form of *quid pro quo.*

"Help with what?"

"You know what." I don't want to specifically say over the phone what it is, and I can tell that Craig is also apprehensive about the prospect that we could be recorded.

"Okay, Andy. I'll look at things and see what I can do as your mayor. Maybe those potholes can be fixed." I take the reply as one that is made to throw off anyone possibly listening in to our conversation. To most, this would be an outlandish thought, but as far as Craig is concerned, there have probably been instances where a court has allowed his phone to be tapped.

"I appreciate it, Craig."

"Anytime, buddy. I'll talk to you later." The phone goes silent before I put the handset back into its cradle on my desk.

"Shit," I say to myself in the quiet of my office.

Chapter Two: Options are Few

A knock on the front door of our house causes us to turn off the television. I get up from my chair as Tori continues to sit quietly, and answer the door. "Hello?"

"Mr. Dixon," a man in uniform says as he stands just outside the threshold of the doorway. "I'm Chief Sean Allen with the Brighton Falls police department. May I come in and have a word with you and Mrs. Dixon?" I step aside and let the officer walk into our home and close the door behind him.

"Chief Allen, what can we help you with?" I ask him as I continue to stand just inside the front door. I met the chief of police several years ago, but only know him as an acquaintance and could never consider him a close friend or confidant. Craig Leighton, however, knows the chief very well.

"I thought I would come over to inform you of something that could be pertinent to you, Mrs. Dixon," he says as he looks at my wife. "As you are already aware, the prosecuting attorney is looking at the city finances." He looks at me and then back at Tori before adding, "From what I am told, there will likely be either an indictment through a grand jury or charges filed directly by the prosecutor's office in the next few days. Therefore, I have been instructed by the court to inform you that you are to remain inside the county until given further instructions." The chief of police pulls an envelope from his pocket and hands it to Tori. "Please consider this your notification that you are not to leave the county without court permission." My wife opens the document and quickly reads it.

"What?" Tori's eyes begin to fill with tears. "Am I under arrest today?"

"No," Chief Allen replies quickly. "This is just a court order that states you are not to leave the county while the investigation is ongoing. Of course, if there is a pressing issue that you would require you to leave the county, such as for medical treatment of some kind, you can contact the phone number on the paperwork I have given you and the court clerk has the authority to either grant the request or deny it." The chief clears his throat. "I apologize for all this. From what I know about the two of you, you are an upstanding couple in the community. I think what Ms. Wood is doing is more of a witch hunt than proper investigative work."

"Can I get you something to drink?" I ask Chief Allen as I can tell there is something else he would like to tell us.

"You know, I wouldn't mind having something to wet my whistle."

"Water? Maybe coffee or tea?"

"Tea," he says with a smile. "It's been a while since I've had some tea." I nod and walk past him toward our small kitchen. As I reach for the ready-made container of cold tea, I begin to pour the chief a glass as he says to us, "The mayor and I have been talking about this whole situation."

"This situation?" Tori wriggles around in her seat as she looks over at me. I pass the cold iced tea over to the officer and have a seat nearby. "Did you talk to Craig, Andy?"

"Yeah, I spoke briefly with him about it. He's of the same opinion as Chief Allen that the new prosecutor is a little out of bounds with this whole investigation." Though I understand that small town politics is a little dirty, I can't be certain how deeply that political muck goes within the police department. We need to be careful what we admit or speak of in front of a representative of the law.

"Mr. Leighton has impressed upon me that we need to keep things above board for now." The chief clears his throat. "Just know that the prosecuting attorney will find herself jumping all sorts of hurdles within my department." A brief smile works its way across his face as he takes a sip of the iced tea I have given him. "Wow, this is pretty good tea. Very sweet."

"Tori makes it," I reply with a smile on my face as I reach over and take her hand. "She is great at everything she does, whether she makes iced tea or balances the sheets in the treasurer's office. Unfortunately, she might have made a mistake on the ledgers that were completely unintentional. I just wish that the prosecutor would see it this way."

"Unlikely," the chief tells me. "Ms. Wood ran on a platform of clearing out any hint of political corruption, and I'm afraid that anyone working within the city government will be targeted at some point. There is more than one hand that is going to appear to be tainted when this is all said and done."

"There are others?" Tori asks as she sits forward on her seat.

The chief nods his head. "I can't share any specifics right now, but it appears that there are quite a few other people in the city as well as in other towns throughout the county who have something to worry about. This new prosecutor acts as if she has something to prove and she is out to do just that."

"Wow." I shake my head as I begin to realize just how deep this could all go. "Is Tori the first one she's targeting?"

"I guess you could say that," the chief admits. "However, she is known for casting a wide net. It's the way she did things in Lanton when she was the city attorney there. There's something about that woman that seems to trigger her to pick a target and then tear into it, no matter what the collateral damage." Chief Allen takes another sip of his iced tea before adding, "Look, I know things can happen. I know that sometimes receipts are lost, or a person can forget and make a personal payment with a city credit card. I'm not going to ask what is going on with you here mainly because I really don't want to know everything. All I really know right now is that the two of you are upstanding community members and Craig Leighton vouches for you both. That's good enough for me right now, and so you have my support." The chief puts his glass down on top of the coffee table in front of him. "I need to get back to the office, though. There are other things to deal with today besides handing you papers and having a drink of tea." He smiles as he stands to his feet and puts his hat back on top of his head.

I stand as well and reach out to shake the officer's hand. "I really appreciate the way you and the mayor have decided to support Tori in this difficult time. It means a lot to the both of us. If you ever need anything, please do not hesitate to ask."

"Thank you very much for that sentiment, Mr. Dixon." The chief turns and walks over to the front door as I follow. He opens it and walks out, and I step out with him as I close the door behind me.

"Chief Allen," I say nervously into the cold air.

"Yes sir?" He turns and looks back at me, his breath visible in the below-freezing conditions.

"Any idea how long it will take to clear this all up for my wife? I'm worried about how it is beginning to affect her emotionally and physically."

The chief of police walks up to me with a sly grin on his face. "Mr. Dixon, let's be totally honest for just a moment, okay? You and I both know that your wife has been bleeding money slowly out of the city's accounts. As a matter of fact, it's something that was being talked about before Ms. Wood even got involved. Mrs. Dixon could have stopped tapping that account way back when the rumors started circulating in town, but she didn't. Instead, it looks like she probably increased her withdrawals as the rumors became more and more plausible. This is not the sort of mess that just goes away overnight."

"Then, why are you here? Why are you helping us if you already believe that Tori is guilty?"

The smirk on the officer's face makes me a bit uneasy as I see him think for a moment. "I think you know where this is going to eventually go, Mr. Dixon. Craig is not a man who will work forever to help you and your wife, no matter how long you have known him. There will be a point at which he will begin to remove his help and then I will have to make a decision as to whether I will continue to do what I can on my end. You and your wife will need to come to the understanding that some sort of arrangement will need to be made with me eventually, whatever that might be." The chief tips his hat and says to me, "Have a good day, Mr. Dixon," before he walks to the street where his car is parked. After I have watched him pull away from the curb and drive away, I turn to go back into the house.

"Shit," I mutter as I go inside.

"What happened?" Tori knows me well enough to know that I went outside with the chief to get a better idea of his view of things.

"It's not good," I reply. "Not good at all, honey." Sitting back down beside my wife, I look into her eyes and ask, "Can you please just be honest with me? How much did you *really* take from the city, Tori?"

My wife looks for a moment as if I have just slapped her in the face with a cold, wet hand. "I can't believe you would ask me something like that, Andy. We have already had this discussion."

"I need to know specifics, dammit," I say to her quietly. "Just give me a better figure than the five thousand dollars you told me yesterday you took out over the last five years. Something doesn't add up here."

Tori takes a quick breath as she looks away. "Can't we just leave this alone? Do I have to air my dirty laundry out to you? It's a fucking job, Andy. You are not my employer."

"Honey, this could take us both down. Financially, I am going to have to figure out how to pay for an attorney to represent you, at least from what the chief has told me. You need to be completely honest with me. How much money did you take?" It's obviously hard for my wife as she struggles to find a way to admit what has been going on for some time in her city office. I think that at this point she realizes that I can no longer be kept in the dark. There are lots of other people who already know the numbers anyway, so it is only a matter of time before I hear the figures as well.

Clearing her throat, my wife answers, "A little more than fifty thousand dollars."

I shake my head as I take a quick, nervous breath. "Holy hell, sweetheart."

"I'm sorry." Tori gets up from her seat and walks back to the bedroom without saying another word. She then closes the door as I sit silently and wonder how she could have pulled ten thousand dollars on average every year out of the city's bank account without anyone knowing.

"We are in deep shit," I mumble as I sit back in my seat. "Deep fucking shit."

Chapter Three: A Tough Position

"Come on in," Mayor Leighton tells us as we stand just outside his office door. Craig has invited the two of us to come have a short meeting with him in his city office. "Close the door please." We do as he asks and then make our way to the two chairs positioned on the side of the desk opposite his chair.

"Thanks for meeting with us today," I say as I sit down beside my wife. "Tori and I are very happy that you and the chief are on the same page."

"The same page. Yes." The mayor looks at the two of us and then back down at a file folder on lying his desk. "I wanted to share something with you that the prosecuting attorney has requested from me. See what you think of it." He turns the folder around and slides it across the desk so that it sits directly in front of Tori. "Do you recognize these accounting entries?"

"I do," my wife replies as she covers her mouth. "Are you really going to give this to her?"

Craig sighs as he leans back in his chair. "I don't know that I have very many other options, Tori. Ms. Wood has been very thorough in her requests to my office, and each time I have been able to comply without any problem. However, this particular ledger entry could have some dire effects on her attempt to build a case against you."

"Is he right?" I ask as I look over at Tori. She nods her head slowly as she looks at the information in front of her. Turning my attention to my old high school classmate, I ask, "Is there not anything that can be done to make this look a little better for my wife? I mean, I know that it's asking a lot, but surely this can be put together in a better light."

"You mean you want me to *fraudulently* change the entries in the ledger," the mayor replies with a sullen look on his face. "That would be just a tad on the illegal side, Andy."

"I'm not asking for anything illegal, *per se,* just something that looks *better.*"

Craig leans on his elbows to look directly at the two of us. "There is no way to make this ledger look any better short of committing at least a half-dozen felonies, Andy. That would put me in jeopardy as well if I were to do that, and I am not all that certain that I can do something like this for your wife."

"Please," Tori says as she looks over at him. "Maybe there is some money that can be moved around or maybe the bank could..."

"Let me stop you right there," the mayor says as he puts a hand up in my wife's direction. "I am not about to walk into the bank and ask for a loan to cover more than fifty thousand dollars' worth of a hole, Tori. That would be a huge indicator for the prosecuting attorney that I am trying to cover something up in her investigation. I am not going to prison over something like this." He sighs while shaking his head. "Besides, there will be an election coming up in November and I am on the ballot again. I can't be thought of as too soft on corruption or else I will not win re-election."

"I know there has to be some way," I tell him. "Everyone in town has seen you get out of some really tight spots with the law."

Craig grimaces. "I have never done anything illegal, Andy. What you are asking me to agree to do would be an illegal act, and once that is done, there is no coming back. I could ruin my life very quickly just to attempt to keep your wife's dealings hidden." The mayor sits back in his chair as he looks at Tori. "Do you still have the money? We might be able to sneak it back into the account if you have it."

"All gone," she says as she puts a hand over her face. "There is nothing left."

"What have you been buying?" I ask my wife as I struggle to understand where that kind of money could have gone so quickly.

"Not now," she tells me as she looks up at the mayor. "Is there anyone who could loan the money to me? I could pay it back with interest after this is all over."

Craig shakes his head. "You would be a very bad bet, Tori. I don't know of a single person who would be willing to fork over that kind of money with simply a promise of repayment sometime in the future. Besides, if someone offered to give you money to help you conceal a crime, they would be guilty of a conspiracy. There could be jail time for them as well."

"Please," Tori says to him as she leans forward against his desk. "Surely there is something that can be done."

Mayor Leighton nods his head slowly, his eyes looking toward the top of his desk before he looks back up at us. "I could front this money for you, but I would be taking a huge risk. However, I don't know that there is anything that would convince me to do go ahead and do something like this when the chances that I could get caught in this would be so high."

Tori stands to her feet and walks around the mayor's desk to where he is seated in his chair. "I think I can offer you something." I watch as my wife goes to her knees and begins to unzip Craig Leighton's pants.

"What the *hell?"* I say loudly as I stand to my feet to see my wife working to get the man's penis out of his pants.

"Sit down," Tori tells me as she looks right at me. "Just let me do what I have to do, Andy. Don't fuck this up for me." She then looks up at the mayor and asks, "Will this work as a sort of payment for you to continue helping me?"

Craig looks at me nervously and then back at my wife. "Yeah, this would work." It's all Tori needs to hear before fishing his cock out of his pants. The mayor's staff swells quickly once it is exposed to her eyesight has my wife's hand wrapped around it.

"Shit." It's all I can think to say as I watch Tori move her hand up and down his erect phallus. *"Shit."*

"This is nice," the mayor tells her as she milks his penis slowly. "It's been a while since I have gotten this sort of attention."

"I've heard you used to have your secretary do this for you." Tori kisses the end of the mayor's cock just as a dribble of pre-come oozes from the hole. "Did that really happen?"

Again, the man looks at me before turning his attention to my wife. "We scratched each other's backs," he admits. "She got what she wanted, and I got what I wanted. It was a nice arrangement."

"I'll bet." Tori slowly goes down on Mayor Leighton, her mouth engulfing his manhood slowly as she takes his full length into her mouth.

"Fuck," Craig says as he sits back in his chair. "Oh, it's been too long."

"This is crazy." I shake my head as I watch the two of them together. Though it's offensive at the very least, I find myself more than just a little interested to watch. "Tori, I can't believe you would do this. You have never been the sort of woman to go out on a limb like this."

The mayor looks at me and asks, "Did you ever think she would take money illegally?"

He has a point as I sit back in my chair. "This is not the way to get what you need, honey."

"I'll front the money and put it in the city account, Andy. Just let her finish me off and I'll do it today and get the prosecutor off her back for a while." He wriggles around in his chair. "Holy shit, she's deepthroating me." I look to see Tori bobbing her head up and down on his cock, taking the full length of his seven inches or so into her mouth. My wife gags a little occasionally, a bit of pre-come mixed with saliva making its way to the mayor's balls.

"Ack...UTT!!!" For a moment I believe that Tori might cause herself to vomit as she gives the man a better blow job than I have ever had from her in ten years of marriage. *"URP!!!"*

"Dammit, Tori," I complain as I scowl in her direction. I watch as her face turns red while she pushes the end of Craig Leighton's cock to the back of her throat. It must feel like heaven to the mayor of our small town. I just wish I knew what deepthroat is like from my own wife.

"Oh, I'm close," the mayor moans as he grips the arm rests of his office chair tightly with his hands. "So fucking close..."

"Wait, are you going to spit or swallow?" I doubt that I will get a verbal response from Tori as I watch her continue to bob up and down on Craig's rod.

"Fuck...*fuck!*" Craig lurches forward a little as he begins to fire his jism into my wife's mouth. *"Ahhh! UHHH!!!"* His face turns just as red as Tori's as he comes inside her throat. To my surprise, my wife is able to capture every spurt of the mayor's white man sauce as he empties his balls into her oral cavity. *"Shit!!!"*

For several seconds, Mayor Leighton pumps his semen into Tori's soft mouth before he begins to relax in his chair. My wife, for her part, pulls her mouth from off the man's penis and swallows his load completely. "You never swallow for me," I protest.

"More than fifty thousand dollars," Tori replies as she wipes her face with a tissue from the mayor's desk. "Give me that kind of money and I will swallow for you too."

I look down and can see that I am hard after seeing my wife suck off the mayor of our small town. Still, I feel a bit cheated since she does not offer to suck me off very often and she rarely swallows when she does it for me. Craig has gotten something from my wife that even I cannot get. "So, what now?" I ask while giving my wife a dour look.

Mayor Leighton slips his dick back into his pants as he says, "I can transfer the money by tomorrow afternoon. Then, I can have the account amended to show that the gap is covered."

"Thank you," Tori says as she comes back to her chair. I don't look over at her immediately, but I can smell the other man's semen on her breath.

"We should go," I say after a brief silence. "It would not look very good for us to spend too much time here with Craig."

"Agreed," the mayor says with a smile. "I will see you both later, then." He stands to his feet and escorts us to his office door. As we leave, I can't help but look at him with a measure of contempt after what he had Tori to do for him.

"What the fuck, Tori?" I say to my wife as we leave the building.

She gives an odd chuckle before replying, "It had to be done, Andy. It's the way things work around here anyway."

"Giving a guy a blow job is the way things work around here? Are you sure that's something you want to be a part of?"

"As opposed to what?" my wife asks angrily. "If I were to go to prison, it could be for five or ten years, Andy. What then? I would be reduced to living behind concrete walls for a large portion of my life and fingering other women to keep from getting the shit kicked out of me while I am there. If a five-minute blow job helps to keep me out of there, I'm more than happy to oblige him."

"You told me you thought of him as being slimy and dishonest, Tori. You said that to me just the other day."

"Sucking his dick doesn't mean that I have changed my mind, honey. He's still a slimy, disgusting character, but a woman does what a woman has to do." We get into the car as I struggle to understand the kind of women my wife has become.

"This is not you, Tori. It never has been."

As I start the car, she looks at me and replies, "Well, maybe it is now." We drive away from city hall, the rest of the trip home relatively quiet as we both reflect upon the line that has now been crossed.

Chapter Four: Legal Haggling

I answer the front door of our house for the second time in three days to see chief of police Sean Allen standing there. He doesn't ask to enter our home this time, but instead just walks right in. "I need to see your wife, please," he says with a grim expression on his face.

"Okay," I say as I try to figure out what's going on. "Give me a moment." I walk back to our bedroom to find Tori and tell her that she needs to come to the living room. She does, smiling widely at the middle-aged officer when she sees him.

"Good afternoon, Chief Allen." He says nothing, but reaches out toward my wife and takes hold of her wrist, whipping her body around quickly and placing a pair of handcuffs on her before either of the two of us can say anything. *"Wait!"*

"What's going on?" I say loudly at the officer.

He turns his eyes toward me and commands, "Sit down and shut up!" Though I want to take a swing at him, I know better that to do something so ridiculous. Chief Allen is armed and probably more than willing to make an example out of me if I try to impede whatever he is up to. As he finishes getting the handcuffs adjusted, he asks, "Are they too tight?"

Tori, crying now as he moves her around briskly, shakes her head. "Why are you doing this?"

The chief takes her to a chair across the living room away from me and sets her down. "I have just heard about what happened at the mayor's office yesterday," he tells us with a certain level of contempt. "Do the two of you have any idea how bad this makes all of us look? The fucking prosecutor is watching *everyone!"* The chief shakes his head as he runs a hand through his hair. "I can't believe the mayor even allowed that to happen."

"I think it was what he was expecting anyway," I tell him coarsely. "He was more than happy to have Tori do that to him."

The chief leans forward in his chair to look me in the eyes. "You met with him at city hall where all of this investigation is taking place.

If you had been a little smarter about it, the two of you could have met in a neutral location, like a hotel outside of town. Instead, I now have a prosecuting attorney breathing down my neck to do something about the collusion that she thinks is rampant in the city government." He shuffles around in his seat. "Dammit, this makes my job even more difficult, you know that?"

I nod my head as I say in a conciliatory tone, "Look, we didn't go there looking to do that with him. The mayor made it clear that he expected something from Tori or else he would have to drop his support for her. She had to do something."

"Well, that *something* has put a wrench in the works." The officer looks over at Tori and asks, "Just what do you think you got for doing that to him? People are starting to hear about these things that you are up to and it's not going to make my job any easier when I have to uphold the law."

"Am I under arrest?" Tori inquires meekly.

"Not yet," Chief Allen replies. "We have to get some things straight." He looks down for a moment as he runs a hand through his thick, pepper-and-salt hair. "I am really putting myself on the line for you and then I hear that Craig is getting all the fun for doing what he his doing. How does that seem fair to you?"

"What?" I shake my head. "Are you asking my wife for a blow job?"

"No," he responds immediately. The chief looks at my wife on the sofa and tells us, "A blow job just wouldn't do it for me." He stands to his feet. "Okay, do you want to keep me on your team or are you ready to face the prosecutor on your own?"

Tori looks up at him. "What do you want me to do?"

The chief smiles a little as he reaches down and helps Tori to her feet. He moves her to the edge of the sofa and faces her toward it before pushing her over the arm. My wife has a pair of soft blue shorts on, the sort she always lounges around in at the end of the day, so it doesn't take much for him to pull them down around her ankles. "Nice undies," he tells her as he pulls on them as well, taking down the crème colored satin panties.

"Fuck," Tori says with surprise as she looks over at me.

"Maybe she doesn't want to do that," I say to the chief of police as I look on nervously.

"No, I'm willing to do it," my wife tells me as she looks back at the officer. "I can't do this alone, Andy. I need some help from the inside, so if this is what it takes, I'm okay with doing this." Tori tries to smile, but I can see that she is as nervous as hell about the fact that the town's highest law enforcement officer is looking at her small ass and muff.

"You are a fine young lady," he tells her as he slides a couple of his fingers along her wet valley. I get a little hard as I watch Chief Allen play with my wife's pussy, her body quivering as he makes pass after pass over her swelling clitoris.

"Shit, honey," I say as I get hard. Trying to avoid getting too bound up, I move my cock around inside my pants to allow for a little extra growth.

The chief pulls his own manhood out from his black trousers and gently moves it around Tori's ass and labia. "Damn," he says as he handles himself. "You are really wet, aren't you, Mrs. Dixon?" He smiles as he presses his cock against my wife's pussy, pushing it in slowly as he pulls up on her tee shirt to reveal her back a bit better.

"Can't you at least take the cuffs off her?" I ask him.

"No," he replies. "I like her being like this." The police chief begins to thrust in and out of my wife, her labia moving in rhythmic motion as his long shaft rakes along them. "You are *really* tight, Mrs. Dixon."

"Holy fuck," Tori says as she tries to keep her head lifted off the sofa cushion. With her wrists fastened together, she is having a difficult time holding herself steady as he humps her.

"Oh, this is good." I watch as the chief fucks my wife deep, his long cock stroking all the way out and then all the way back in. He is enjoying every inch of Tori's short vagina, undoubtedly hitting her cervix squarely as she grimaces with each thrust.

"You're not going to come inside her, are you?" I ask as I watch him fuck my wife.

"Not sure," he says. "Is she fertile?"

"I don't know," Tori tells him. "Please, not in my pussy." Her dark brown hair falls over her face and onto the sofa as she continues to be pounded from behind.

"It won't take me long," Chief Allen tells us. "I haven't had good pussy in a long time. My wife doesn't put out much anymore." He grunts a couple of times as he gets closer to having an orgasm. "Fuck, I wish my wife would let me fuck her like this." The chief's motions become harder as he grips Tori's hips tightly, pulling her against him hard every time he pushes his cock into her. "Damn, I can feel the end of your hole."

"Uh huh," my wife replies as she clenches her fists behind her back.

"Fuck..." I can tell that the chief is about to spunk inside Tori. *"Fuck..."* Suddenly, he pulls out of her pussy and rams his cock into my wife's handcuffed, soft hands behind her back. *"Ohhh!!! OHHH!!!"* The chief of police for Brighton Falls begins to ejaculate into my wife's soft hands as she grips him tightly behind her back. *"Uhhhh! Mmmmm..."* He continues to thrust and spurt, his jism shooting through her wrapped fingers and across her lower back. *"Shit...oh..."* The chief keeps moving his cock in and out of my wife's hands until he finishes losing his load all over her. Chief Allen pulls his penis out of Tori's hands and gets a handcuff key from his belt. He takes off the handcuffs before he even bothers to stuff his wilted manhood back into his pants.

"Thank goodness," I say as I look at the mess in Tori's hands and along her back.

"Yeah, he didn't come inside me. That was a good thing." My wife stands up and cleans off her hands before she gets her shorts and underwear pulled back up so that she can come back over to me.

"Here's the deal," the officer says after getting his johnson put away. "Don't leave me out of any deals, okay? I'm here too and even though the mayor can help you both out some, I can help in many other ways. Besides, the prosecuting attorney may soon stop going directly to Mayor Leighton if she has her way."

"Why?" I ask as my wife sits down beside me, the smell of sex all over her.

"He is one of the subjects of the investigation now, as far as I can tell. The prosecutor is looking to find a means by which she can go after him without tipping all the other mayors in the county off to the fact that she is after him."

"Wow." I look at Tori and can see that this information does not completely surprise her. City government, after all, has quite a few others vying for the use of public funds.

"That's what you meant by the fact that there are other *hands* in this. The mayor and some others have been doing something, right?"

The chief nods his head as he replies, "I can't really get too far into any detail. Suffice it to say, Mr. Leighton has dug his own hole, and I think he might try to use you to get out of it." The town's head police officer goes to our front door and opens it slowly as he adds, "Remember, you are not allowed to leave the county without special permission from the court. Keep a low profile and I will contact you if there is anything important I am able to relay to you."

I nod toward him as he leaves, closing the door behind him. "What an asshole," I say to my wife when I am certain the officer has gotten away from our front door. "Are you alright?" I ask Tori.

"Fine," she replies calmly. "I'm worried, Andy. How many people are really involved in this? What if this is much bigger than what I have been doing at city hall?"

"It could be much, *much* bigger," I concur. "But you have to be careful who you talk to about this. There could be money coming out of city hall that will be traced eventually to all sorts of people in city government. We can't be certain that there won't be an attempt by someone else to get you into a shady agreement with them."

"If one card falls, the whole house comes down," Tori says as she looks at me. "This is a house of cards. If just one is pulled out, we all suffer the consequences." Though I hate the thought that there could be a very large financial coverup whereas Tori's misdeeds are just the tip of the iceberg, it does seem to make sense. We will have to keep our heads down, just as suggested by the chief of police, if we want to keep ourselves as far out of this as possible. However, that doesn't mean we won't have to deal with the other cards. We could very well be in for the long haul with several others who are trying to avoid the prosecuting attorney's sharp eyes.

Sign up to my Patreon account and receive exclusive Hotwife stories every month and sexy scenes every week!

https://www.patreon.com/karlyviolet

Chapter Five: Not Exactly Marital Bliss

"It's the attorney," Tori says to me as she hangs up the phone.

"How much?" I knew this was coming when we first had a so-called free consultation meeting with the criminal defense attorney concerning the pending charges in the case against my wife.

"Two hundred per hour," she replies before adding, "They want three thousand dollars upfront for their retainer fee."

"Dammit," I say with clenched teeth. "We don't have that, Tori."

"The furniture store." My wife looks at me as if what I have just said doesn't make sense to her. "Just borrow the money from the business."

I shake my head. "The store isn't like the city government's offices where money is sitting there ripe for the taking, honey. I have to *earn* that money, and the store's resources are not my own. There isn't even that much money in the bank account for the store right now anyway."

"How much is in it? We could give them whatever is in the store's account and maybe they will allow us to make payments beyond that."

"Tori, there might be a little more than two thousand dollars in the furniture store's account, but I can't just take it out for personal use. I would have to pay myself with it, deduct all applicable income taxes, and so on. The amount we would get would be a little more than a thousand dollars after all of that. It's just not worth it."

"You don't have to pay yourself, Andy! Trust me, all you need to do is just pull it and come up with an accounting trick that shows it as being paid out for services to the store. You need some extra painting done inside, right? Well, use the money to *hire* a paint crew that expects a cash payment."

"The receipt," I say incredulously. "There has to be a receipt when you make those sorts of claims on the tax forms."

"You can make receipts yourself." My wife looks at me as if this is as easy as a stroll in the park. Of course, she has been doing this or something like it for a while at city hall.

I level my eyes at her and reply, "Look, you have gotten yourself into a hell of a lot of trouble by doing that sort of thing at your job as city treasurer, remember? I am not about to do the same thing at my own business and then hope to hell that the federal government won't catch me cheating on my tax returns. That's all I would need in my life right now is to not only have to find money to defend you from what you have done, but then to have to defend myself in court!" My tongue is sharp as I say this all to my wife, and a part of me feels terribly for being to mean. However, she should know better at this point after being suspended from city hall pending criminal charges in the case.

"Sell the fucking store, Andy. It's nothing but a millstone around our necks. Get rid of it."

"Are you kidding? My dad started that store forty years ago and put his heart and soul into it, Tori. He worked hard to bring it up from a small breadcrumb business to one that actually earns a bit more money than we should have ever needed. It was supposed to be our nest egg."

"It doesn't earn shit, Andy! It needs to go!"

"It's the only fucking thing bringing money into our home now, Tori!" I slam my fist down on the dining room table as I stare back at my wife. "You have basically lost your job because you wanted a few nicer things."

"I told you I was paying the electric bill and some of the other bills we had."

"Bullshit, Tori. You have been buying some nicer things for yourself, like two-hundred-dollar pairs of shoes, while I have been paying myself from the store more and more to cover the things that you at one time would use your paycheck to cover. You have had to take money to cover the electric bill because you had already spent all your regular paycheck on shit that we did not need in order to make ends meet. You got greedy, Tori. That's all there is to it." There have been several people so far tell my wife the same thing. She was greedy, and in the process, she stole so much money that it was no longer easy to hide the effect. It's how someone in the city treasurer's office noticed that money was missing and it's how the prosecuting attorney found out.

"You're an asshole," she says quietly to me. "A fucking asshole who doesn't give a shit for his wife."

"I *do* give a shit," I tell her as I sit back in my chair. "The problem is that you don't want to admit how far into the hole we are." I stare forward for a moment before adding, "This attorney will cost more than that three thousand dollars, Tori. That's just the tip of the iceberg. By the time this is all said and done, the cost will likely be over ten thousand. If you lose the case and we then are forced to file an appeal, that could be another ten thousand or so. Get the picture?" I look coldly over at Tori. "That fifty thousand dollars you took from the city is going to have to be returned as well. You know that will be a part of anything that happens, even if you get some sort of plea deal. Every fucking penny will have to be repaid and there is no way you would be allowed to bankrupt yourself out of it." I fold my hands and look away from Tori. "Maybe I should sell the store. They are going to end up taking it anyway by the time this is all over anyway."

"You care about that store more than you do for me," she sulks. Tori sits down in a chair across the table from me. "You would choose that store over me if you were pushed to make that decision."

"That's where you are wrong, my dear." I try to soften my tone as I look over at my wife. "I would sacrifice the store for you if it would help. Unfortunately, it won't." I lean forward as I shake my head. "I've already had the store appraised in hopes that I could get a loan on the value of it, and it only has a value of eighty thousand dollars right now. Even if I got that loan, it would have to be paid back at some point in the future."

"But the business is worth so much more."

"Sure, it is, but you are talking about trying to *sell* it. Nobody in this town wants to buy my store. It's not in the part of town that is currently growing, and it isn't a huge moneymaker at this time. Tori, I have asked around to see if I could sell it, and the local real estate companies are not interested in representing me without a very large commission. They tell me it won't sell easily enough for them to ask for anything less."

Tori begins to cry, her hands going to her face as she considers the fact that we have our backs to the wall and do not have the funds required to mount a reasonable defense in her case. "That prosecutor is going to fuck me over, Andy. She's out for blood, and she won't stop until she has nailed me to the wall."

There has been a lot of talk in town about how persistent the new prosecuting attorney is when asking questions of potential witnesses. Patricia Wood is a thorough practitioner of the law, calculating and resilient in everything that she does. From what I have heard, she was a lot like this when she started out as a criminal defense attorney. She learned every trick of the trade when it came to keeping clients out of prison, and apparently, she has turned that knowledge around to use it to keep other attorneys from helping their own clients. It really doesn't seem all that fair on face value, but there it is.

"We'll keep working on getting more money in somehow, Tori. I'm planning to have a huge sale at the store anyway, so maybe I can get enough customers in to pay myself a bonus that is large enough to cover the retainer fee." Tori looks up at me and tries to smile at first, but soon buries her face back into her hands. Though she has brought this mess upon herself and our household, I can't help but have some sympathy for my wife. I do love her very much, even though I am still angered that she put us into this mess to begin with.

"Thank you, honey," she says as she gets up from her seat and comes over to me. Tori embraces me tightly and I hold her as she cries. "I wish I could find a way to help you make the money."

"You could always pimp yourself out." Though I intend it as a joke, she steps back from me and looks down as if I have attempted to plunge a knife into her back.

"Are you fucking kidding me, Andy? Why would you say something like that?"

"Honey, I was joking around with you. I don't mean anything by it, I swear." I try to give Tori a sweet smile, but it seems to only exacerbate her anger.

"You are a fucking asshole, Andy, just like I said before. A self-absorbed, selfish *asshole.*"

"Self-absorbed? *Selfish?!*" I stand from my seat as I face off with Tori. "I just told you that I have looked into trying to get a loan on the store to pay for your attorney and I am doing what I can to make more money while you are suspended without pay from your job at city hall. How the hell does that make me selfish, Tori? How the hell can you make *me* out to be the bad person in this relationship when I am not the one who put us in this hell hole to begin with?" Shaking my head, I walk over to the front door and get my set of car keys. "Fuck you, Tori. Fuck you and your sorry attitude!" I walk out and slam the door behind me before going to my car.

How did this just happen? Tori and I were sharing a tender moment a few minutes ago after a tussle about the store and her potential attorney fees. How the hell could I have told her to pimp herself out? How could she have taken it so *seriously?* Right now, all I can do is look back at what a terrible decision it was to toss the joke at Tori. My wife and I could be on the way to separating soon if things do not begin to look up.

Chapter Six: A Nervous City Council

We have been asked by the mayor to attend tonight's city council meeting, so my wife and I have decided that it would be in her best interest to do so, especially considering that the city council could at some point decide to fire my wife. "Thank you for agreeing to meet with us in executive session," Mayor Craig Leighton says as he looks just briefly at my wife. He remembers very well what Tori did for him in his office a couple of weeks ago to secure his continued support in the ongoing investigation into the city's finances. "The council members have a few questions for the two of you, so we felt it would be best to keep the general public out of the meeting since this concerns a personnel matter." The mayor looks over at one of the council members and asks, "Mr. Childers, I believe you are supposed to head this up?"

"Yes, Mayor Leighton," he replies with a grim look on his face. Lloyd Childers is the oldest person on the council, almost eighty years of age, and is a former dentist in our small town. Both Tori and I have been to see Dr. Childers in the past as children, but he has been retired for about fifteen years now. The older gentleman seems to pass most of his time nowadays by working as a city councilman and visiting the local barbershop for the town's gossip. The latter is probably the biggest reason why he is in charge of the line of questioning the council has decided to pursue.

"Mr. and Mrs. Dixon, you are here tonight because there are questions regarding the nature of your handling of the current investigation into the city's missing funds." Dr. Childers stares over at us before asking, "Mrs. Dixon, what are you doing with your time now that you are on unpaid suspension from your position as city treasurer?"

"What am I doing?" Tori looks over at me and I shrug my shoulders. "Well, I guess I am sitting at home and waiting for something to happen with the whole thing. I've not heard from the prosecutor or from anyone else involved, so I don't know what to expect or whether I should just go look for another job."

"Another job," Dr. Childers says with a slight snarl. "Are you presently employed anywhere else?"

"No," Tori replies.

"There are rumors going around that you have found other ways to bring in an income during the investigation, Mrs. Dixon." Dr. Childers clears his throat. "Some of these rumors are a bit disturbing, in my estimation."

"What are you talking about?" I ask as I sit forward in my seat. "What rumors?"

"Mr. Dixon, I think what Councilman Childers is alluding to is the rumor that you and your wife are involved in some sort of illegal activity to continue making money." Becky Samuelson is the newest member of the city council, having been elected only last year. She is young and very intelligent, at least judging from what I have seen of her in past council meetings I have attended. Unfortunately, I'm not certain which way she leans as to whether she feels Tori's termination should be permanent.

"There is no illegal activity going on, Ms. Samuelson," I say with confidence. "As you know, I own a furniture store and my wife helps me there since she is not allowed to go back to work in the treasurer's office for now."

Dr. Childers asks, "Have you heard the rumors?"

"What rumors? We are not up to anything that could be considered even slightly illegal, sir. However, if you could tell us to which rumors you are referring, we could attempt to put your mind at ease."

"Mrs. Dixon, do you sell your body for sexual purposes?" The question from the oldest member of the council is so surprising that my jaw drops. I don't know what to say at first as I look over at Tori.

My wife puffs up a bit and looks at the mayor before turning her full attention to Dr. Childers. "You had better be joking, councilman. If you are serious about this..."

"There are *rumors,*" the councilman says again. "I have heard them from four of five reliable sources in town."

"Reliable sources?" I laugh. "Do you mean from the old geezers who get their hair cut downtown? *Those* reliable sources?" There is a bit of snickering from a couple of other council members as Dr. Childers becomes obviously flustered. Rarely is there a person who would dare address the former dentist in the way I have decided to.

"Mr. Dixon, this is a serious matter and I would only use trusted information when asking such questions." He sits back in his chair. "Still, you have not denied the rumor."

"Deny yourself," my wife says as she looks at the older man. "You have no right to ask me something like that, councilman. No right at all. As a matter of fact, to make such a claim in public is slanderous."

"But, Mrs. Dixon, this is a closed executive session. None of the general public are hearing this right now, so there is no slander going on," replies Councilwoman Samuelson. "These are just concerns we have, because the public is hearing these same rumors around town."

"Just because there are rumors does not make a single one of them true," I chime in as I look at the council. "Since when does this council take the time to address rumors? I mean, when was the last time that anyone discussed the rumor about Councilman Smith and his wife Nancy?"

"What are you talking about?" Councilman Smith says as he sits forward at the table.

"You know exactly what I am talking about, Mr. Smith. Last year, there was a rumor that you and your wife were selling marijuana near the school. I don't recall there being an executive session around that time to discuss anything like that."

"Those were *unfounded lies!"* the councilman says as he stands to his feet. "I don't even smoke the stuff, so why would I be selling it?"

"Oh, I don't know," I say with disgust. "Maybe you needed some extra money when you lost your job at the factory that spring?"

"This is not about me or my wife!" he yells out as two other councilmembers try to calm him down.

The mayor uses his gavel, rapping it three times, before saying, "Let's keep this on topic, ladies and gentlemen." Mayor Leighton looks at us and asks, "So, you are basically saying that the rumors are not true, and that the council should move on to more pressing matters, correct?" I can sense by the way Craig phrases his words, he wants to help take the pressure off us. After all, my wife did give him some oral pleasure that has kept him, so far, on our side.

"We are not doing anything illegal," I say plainly. "Anything else besides that is none of your fucking business."

"Language, Mr. Dixon," Dr. Childers scolds as he crosses his arms.

"Begging your pardon, sir, but you just accused my wife of having sex with men for money. So, if I want to tell you that it is none of your *fucking* business what we are doing in our own home, then I am going to say that it is none of your *fucking* business!" I stand to my feet and look at the council as they all seem to take issue with my chosen vocabulary. "Let me make it abundantly clear, ladies and gentlemen, that my wife and I have been through a lot with this pointless investigation already. Tori is innocent of everything that the prosecutor is thinking of throwing at her, and we will prove it very soon when everything is finally concluded. Until then, we are struggling to get by because you have seen fit to suspend my wife for allegations that have yet to be proven. I have no confidence in this council to be fair in any way to Tori or to myself, and so I no longer plan to cooperate with any of you concerning this ongoing witch hunt."

"Witch hunt? There is money missing from the city's accounts, Mr. Dixon. Your wife is the treasurer of this town and she is responsible for the loss of those funds, however they have disappeared."

I look over at the mayor. He had agreed to move more than fifty thousand dollars back into the accounts to help cover Tori's guilt in everything, but I can only assume at this point that he has not done so. Looking at Dr. Childers, I tell him, "If I hear anything being spread by the members of this council concerning Tori or me, I will see to it that you are sued for defamation of character. Ladies and gentlemen, you think you have seen a legal mess, but wait until you get a pissed off furniture salesman after you!"

"Honey." Tori stands up beside me and says to me, "Calm down. You have made your point."

"I think the council has wasted enough of the Dixon's time tonight." The mayor looks over the councilmembers' faces. All are silent as he asks, is there a motion to close this executive session of the city council?"

"I move to close," Councilwoman Samuelson says as she continues to stare at me.

"I second," says another council member who has sat relatively silent for the duration of the meeting.

"All in favor?" The mayor waits for the *aye* votes, receiving enough that when he calls for *nay's* he only gets the one from the former dentist. "This meeting is adjourned." Mayor Leighton raps his gavel three times again and then sits quietly as the councilmembers get up and begin to file out of the room. Tori and I stand there in defiance as we wait for the last one to leave.

"This is a real mess," I tell the mayor as he walks over to us.

"Yes, it is," he replies. "I'm having a very tough time finding ways to put the money into the account without alerting someone that it is happening. The prosecuting attorney has placed a monitor on the city's accounts until the investigation is over."

"She suspects that something could be added back," I say with a grimace on my face.

"Yep." The mayor then looks at my wife to ask, "You haven't been doing anything on the side for money, have you? I mean the sort of thing that Dr. Childers brought up."

Tori looks sullenly at Craig and replies, "Should I include you in my answer to that question?" The answer is biting, causing the mayor to hold up his hands as he backs away, a smug look on his face. He leaves through the same door the councilmembers left through moments ago, leaving us to our thoughts.

"You can't be angry with me forever," I say to my wife as I try to hold her hand.

"I can be angry for as long as I want," she replies without looking at me as she pulls her hand away. "Let's go home."

"Okay, we'll go home. Even so, you need to stop fighting with me all the time, Tori. If we can't present a united front with these people, you will end up losing your job permanently and the prosecutor will be able to get to you much easier. You don't want that, do you?"

"I don't know what I want anymore," my wife says as we walk out of the large meeting room and then down the hallway to the exit at city hall. "These people are going to do whatever they can to bury me in all of this, even though some of them are dirtier than I am."

"It's probably why they are coming after you so hard. Dr. Childers could have had his hands in some of what has been taken from the city's coffers."

"He's practically a millionaire," she tells me as she walks briskly to the car. "The man doesn't want the city's money. He just wants to die with a reputation that he cared enough to try to save the town from its evil treasurer. He's just an..."

"Asshole?" I quip as we get into the car.

Tori shakes her head as she looks over at me. "*You* are an asshole, honey, but I still love you." We kiss for a moment before I start the car. There is nothing in this world as important to me as my wife. I just need her to understand that.

Chapter Seven: An Open Secret

"I hate grocery shopping," Tori tells me as we walk into the local supermarket.

"I know," I reply with some understanding. Over the past few weeks there has been a lot said in the community about the two of us. Grocery stores and other public places in our small town are festering waterholes for such gossip and innuendo. "We still need to be able to eat, and you are not allowed to leave the county without court permission."

"Shit," my wife says under her breath as we walk in. "There's Cynthia Davis."

"Cynthia? Hey, you two are friends, right?"

Tori huffs as she says to me, "We *were* friends at one time, Andy, but she is one of the biggest rumormongers in town."

"Hey, Tori!" the young woman says as she practically skips up to us by the fresh vegetables.

"Cynthia, hello." My wife launches a faux smile that is so realistic that I almost believe the lie it carries in regards to how Tori feels about the sudden meeting between the two women.

"It's been ages since we last spoke. How are the two of you doing?" Cynthia's bright blue eyes look from my wife to me and then back again as she attempts to engage us in the sort of warm back-and-forth that at one time I enjoyed.

"We're fine," my wife replies. "How are you and Stan?"

"Stan is wonderful," the woman says as she picks up a head of cabbage and places it into her cart. "He's still working over at the retirement home." Cynthia's husband has a degree in hospital administration but took the head job at the retirement home several years ago so that his wife could be closer to family. There was a time when he and I were on close speaking terms, but that ended a couple of years back when he accused me of selling him broken furniture. I replaced the end table that apparently had a manufacturing defect and I thought that was all there would be to it. Unfortunately, Mr. Davis then felt the need to tell others that I had been intentionally defrauding others out of their money by selling inferior furniture. This lie has cost me some business over time.

"And your son?"

"Anson is doing well. He just enrolled in college this past fall and he is working on a degree in business economics."

"Wonderful." It seems as if Tori is beginning to settle into the conversation with Cynthia. Maybe even though so much has been floating around the community about us this will be something or someone that my wife can finally cling to for a little support.

"So, I've heard things, Tori." My hopes are suddenly dashed with the impromptu statement.

"Things?" Tori looks down at her feet as she crosses her arms and then back up at Cynthia.

"You know, it's all just talk, I'm certain. But still, you probably should hear about it from me instead of from someone else."

"What sort of talk, Cynthia?"

The woman shuffles around a little and after looking around at a few other shoppers tending to their own business, she says, "Stan heard some guys at work talking about coming to see you for some kind of *extra* service."

"*Extra service?"* Tori shakes her head. "What do you mean by that?"

"You know," Cynthia says with a strange look on her face. "Like, maybe, sex for money?"

"Your *husband* heard this?" I ask as I feel myself becoming angry.

"Yeah, at work. Oh, no, don't get me wrong, Andy. It's all just talk, I'm sure, but Stan told me about it and we thought that you ought to know."

"He's a liar," I blurt out as I take my wife's hand into mine. "Anything that comes out of your husband's mouth can't be trusted any further than I can throw his fat ass."

"Andy!" My wife looks up at me as she squeezes my hand.

Looking down at her, I reply, "I'm sorry, honey, but Stan didn't hear this from other guys and then just feel like it was his civic duty to get that information to us through his dear wife. He's been spreading this along with his buddies for the past week or more. They are all in on this."

"You have no right to..." I don't allow Mrs. Davis to finish her thought as I put my hand up near her face.

"I don't even want to hear it from you, Cynthia. This rumor mill that is churning in the community is ridiculous." I step close to her and ask, "What else have you heard or said about Tori and me? I know there must be more getting chatted about all over the town. After all, it gets boring saying the same thing all the time, right?"

The woman backs away from me, a perplexed look on her face. "I can't believe that you honestly want to attack me like this. All I am doing is letting you know that things are being said."

"Of course, they are. The only problem is, there are people like you and your husband who are keeping this going. Tori and I are not doing anything illegal, and we are working hard to just stay afloat. Why can't you people see that?"

"Honey, stop." Tori pulls softly on my arm. "Let's just get what we need and get out of here."

"You should listen to your wife," Cynthia remarks snidely. "Maybe then the two of you would have less time for entertaining men in your home."

"Excuse me?" Tori looks at her old friend. "I don't do that, Cynthia."

"Men have told Stan that you do. They say you give blow jobs for a hundred dollars and full sex for two hundred. There are a lot of guys saying this, Tori. How can you say that it's not happening if there are so many who claim they have been to see you?"

"Fuck!" My wife's face becomes contorted as she walks right up to Cynthia. "Tell that filthy husband of yours that I didn't want to suck

his dick because of the sores that were all over it. I'm sorry I turned him down, but I have to keep my health in mind when I do that."

My heart jumps as I watch Cynthia's face become white. "Stan came to you for sex?"

"I told him I wouldn't do it because he had three or four sores all over his penis, Cynthia. I don't know what he is carrying, but I don't want anything to do with that." There are two shoppers nearby who I am certain hear my wife's comment. They have stopped their carts and are pretending to look at some of the other produce in the aisle as my wife caps it off, "Herpes is no laughing matter. I'm not going to do anything with a guy who has warts or sores on his johnson."

"Shit," I say under my breath as Tori turns and gives me a quick wink.

"No, not my Stan. He wouldn't do that." There is a distraught look on the woman's face as she looks for a moment at us and then at the shoppers nearby. Quietly but quickly, she pushes her cart along the aisle toward the checkout at the front of the store.

"What have you done?" I say quietly to my wife so as to keep the other shoppers from hearing me.

"I turned the tables on them, Andy. I am so damned tired of being on the defensive all the time. It's time that I start being more proactive." My wife takes my hand and we continue down the store aisle to grab whatever else is on our list.

"That was all a lie, right?"

"Of course, it was," Tori says with a grin on her face. "But it was one that will keep Cynthia off my back while she goes after Stan. He will wish that he wasn't spreading things about me before this is all over."

"Wow, honey," I say as we continue to shop. "I wasn't sure you had it in you."

"I wasn't either," Tori replies. "The time has come to do something about what is happening to me now, though. I will no longer just sit and be the victim. If that bitch of a prosecutor wants a fight, I'll give her a fight." I bend down to give Tori a quick kiss as I smile to myself. Maybe finally we can work on clearing things up together.

Chapter Eight: An Accounting Error

"I'm nervous," Tori says as we get out of the car and walk toward the front entrance of the courthouse. "This is getting far too real, honey."

"I know," I reply as I pat her on the shoulder. "Mr. Millhouse says that this is fairly standard and that there will be a lot of questions that you simply will not have to answer."

"Plead the Fifth," my wife says with a shaky voice.

"Plead the Fifth," I confirm. "The attorney will tell you when to assert that right as well as when to answer a question. Keep in mind that the prosecuting attorney will try to trick you into saying something incriminating, so be careful."

"Hello, Mrs. Dixon. Mr. Dixon." The young lawyer was not the one we originally hoped to retain, but is the best we can afford at the moment. The three thousand dollars that the other, more-experienced attorney wanted just wasn't possible for us, so we turned to a fairly new attorney who was willing to accept one thousand to show up and represent us for this deposition as well as for court. He expects another thousand by next month, so I will have to work extra hard to get that money from the furniture store somehow.

"Good morning, Mr. Millhouse," I say with what must be an uneasy smile. "We are here and ready to get this over with today."

The young man of thirty looks at me and then at my wife as he smiles. "This should not be so bad today, I would not think. Just be very careful about what you say or how you say anything. If you do not understand a question, ask and it will be explained a bit better. Ms. Wood is a tough prosecutor from what I have seen, but she knows she is not allowed to badger you into some sort of confession. Even so, don't give her anything that she could bring up in court." Mr. Millhouse reaches out and pats my wife on the side of her arm. "Just try to relax and remain calm. We will all get through this together." The young attorney turns around and begins to lead us through the courthouse to one of the conference rooms along the bottom floor of the three-story county building. As we walk together, I think about what Mr.

Millhouse has said and how it all sounds like a canned speech. I smile strangely to myself as I think about all that he went through to make it to where he is today, making one-third the money as any other attorney in town until he can make a name for himself. This could be his one shot. If he gets my wife out from underneath the prosecutor's thumb, even I will shout his name to the world. My wife would become his greatest walking advertisement.

"It's such a big room," Tori says as she trembles at my side. I pull her close to me as we walk in, three people already waiting for us inside. One of them, a woman in her latter thirties who is very well-dressed, stands on the side of the table opposite the door. I assume instantly that she will be our greatest foe.

"Welcome to the chamber, Mr. and Mrs. Dixon," the woman says as she extends a hand. "I am Patricia Wood, Chief Prosecutor for the county." I am the first to reach out and shake her hand, a strange thing in my estimation to do when I consider that she is actively trying to find a way to put my wife in prison and throw away the key.

Tori looks at her hand and says, "Sorry, but I just don't think I can do it." She then takes a seat next to where our attorney is standing as he shakes the prosecutor's hand.

"I understand," the tall woman says with a smile before sitting down herself. "There is good reason to be nervous, Mrs. Dixon, but I assume Mr. Millhouse has prepared you for today?"

My wife looks over at her attorney, who nods his head. "Yes." It's a simple and straight response, the sort of one that Mr. Millhouse cautioned Tori to make every single time. No additional information is offered, so no additional information is available for Ms. Wood's consideration.

"Good," the prosecuting attorney responds. "Let's get started then, shall we?" She nods her head toward one of the people with her and that person presses a button on a camera that is sitting to one side of the table. "This is inquiry number seven-two-four, and the date is the

Sixth of January." Ms. Wood clears her throat as she continues, "My name is Patricia Wood, Chief Prosecuting Attorney. To my left is Mr. Clarence Dodd, my technical aide for this meeting today, and to my right is Mrs. Janice Clausen, Deputy Prosecuting Attorney. With us today is Mr. Andrew Dixon and Mrs. Tori Dixon along with their legal representative, Mr. Thomas Millhouse, Esquire."

My wife continues to shake a little as I pull her close to me while the camera continues to record us. "Ms. Wood, as defense counsel, I would like to state on the record that my client will be asserting throughout the majority of the deposition today her right to refuse to self-incriminate. On par, I would also like to state that Mr. Dixon, my client's legal spouse, will also be exercising his right under state and federal statutes to refuse to answer any questions that deal with anything the State believes could lead to charges against Mrs. Dixon." With apparent practiced form, the delivery of our attorney's opening statement seems to be pretty solid. I feel less apprehensive now about his ability to move us through this morass.

"Very well, Mr. Millhouse. We will assume that the Dixon's will attempt to avoid self-incrimination. However, I must tell you that there are other people involved in this case as potential suspects, and so it is my duty to ask difficult questions that could reflect guilt in another party. Your clients do not have the right under the law to refuse direct questions concerning another party's guilt or innocence. I assume this is made clear?"

"Very clear," the young attorney replies immediately.

"Alright then. Let us begin." The prosecuting attorney shuffles through a file folder and asks the first question. "Mrs. Dixon, how long have you worked for the city?"

Mr. Millhouse nods his head, so Tori answers, "Eight years."

"Were all of those years as the treasurer?"

Again, my wife waits to see our attorney nod his head. "No."

"How many years have been as the city's treasurer." Ms. Wood looks sharply at my wife as Tori looks at Mr. Millhouse. "You realize that you don't have to get permission from him to answer all of the questions, don't you?"

"She will continue to seek my counsel, Ms. Wood, on everything that is asked, not just the mundane." I'm suddenly even more impressed with the young man's tenacity. He doesn't back down on inch as he looks back across the table at the prosecuting attorney.

"Understood," Ms. Wood replies. "How many years as treasurer, Mrs. Dixon?"

After seeing Mr. Millhouse give her the go-ahead, my wife answers, six years."

"Six years," the prosecutor says as she focuses her light blue eyes in the direction of my wife. "You only held a job with the city for two years before getting such a very important position like treasurer?"

"Don't answer that," Mr. Millhouse says before Tori can even look at him.

"And why not?" Ms. Wood asks.

"You're baiting her," he replies. "My client has already answered your questions concerning her length of tenure with the city. You can do your own math."

A sly grin comes across the tall woman's face as she looks at the young man sitting beside us. I'm not sure whether I should take her appearance as a sign that she is amused or that she is angry with him and therefore with us. Either way, there is a slight uptick in her voice as she replies, "I suppose you are correct, Mr. Millhouse. My apologies." The prosecuting attorney turns to look at the deputy prosecutor. "Do you have those records from April and May of last year?"

"I do," she replies. The older woman reaches into a file box and removes a thin folder, placing it on the table in front of the prosecuting attorney.

"Thank you," she says as she opens it up and looks at the first page. "Mrs. Dixon, are you aware that money is missing from the city treasury?"

My wife almost answers, but Mr. Millhouse puts his hand on top of hers. "You are alleging there is money missing, Ms. Wood. Whatever Mrs. Dixon has heard concerning your case is not a pertinent part of her testimony."

"I think it is," she retorts. "Is she going to refuse to answer?" The prosecutor's eyes lock onto my wife's. "There is nothing about this that could incriminate you, Mrs. Dixon. You can answer a question about whether you have *heard* of something. It's not as if you are saying that you are the responsible person for the disappearance, is it?" She smiles warmly, but I can tell that there is a bit of venom in the way she speaks to Tori.

"Our attorney has advised my wife, and I think that is where we will leave that question." Her eyes suddenly turn toward me, and I feel a chill run along the back of my neck.

"I didn't ask you a question, Mr. Dixon. You should keep your responses to only the questions I ask you."

"Oh, I have a few other responses I would love to share with you." My anger flairs a little as I stare down the prosecuting attorney.

"We need to remain calm, Mr. Dixon," Mr. Millhouse says to me. "Let me handle this, okay?" I can sense that the exchange I have had with Ms. Wood makes him a little nervous. He warned us that she might attempt to make my wife and I a bit uncomfortable by testing our boundaries. Now she has found those boundaries and I would hope that she would honor them.

"Fine," Ms. Wood says as she sits back in her seat. "Let me do all of the talking then." She moves more of the pages around in the file folder. "Mrs. Dixon, I have quite a substantial paper trail that seems to point toward you as a prime suspect in the disappearance of more than two hundred thousand dollars from the city accounts."

"Two hundred thousand?" My wife shakes her head as Mr. Millhouse again pats her hand to remind her to be careful of what she says.

"And some change," the prosecuting attorney replies. "I even have data entries that appear to have been made by you that suggest that you are responsible for the vast majority of the improper entries made in the ledgers."

"Mrs. Dixon does not agree that there are improper entries, Ms. Wood," our attorney interjects.

"Perhaps you should allow her to speak to that point? Maybe she could clear up a lot of confusion on the part of my investigators."

"There is no confusion," Mr. Millhouse says to her. "We all understand what the game being played is right now. Threatening my client in this way is beneath your office, Ms. Wood."

"Oh, give me a break, Tom." It's the first time we have heard Ms. Wood use the first name of our attorney, as if they are well acquainted with each other already. "If your client doesn't start helping us out, I will have no choice but to go after her and anyone else connected with her. I can't just sit back and allow these enormous holes in the budget to go without some sort of recompense."

"What are you suggesting, Patricia?" he asks.

The prosecuting attorney nods her head toward Mr. Dodd. He stops the video camera and turns it toward the table top. "Fine, everything is off the record for now."

"Keep your mouth shut and just listen," Mr. Millhouse says as he looks at the two of us. Then, looking across the table at the prosecutor and her deputy, he asks, "What do you have in mind?"

She sighs a little, her long blonde hair moving up and down with her chest as she breathes steadily. "Admission that there is negligence on her part as well as some attempt to cover up for other people who have been actively draining money from the city accounts. In return, I will ask the judge to accept a plea deal that would allow a misdemeanor charge of official corruption and negligence with a sentence of two to five years in the county lockup. Fifty thousand dollars in restitution would also be requested in order to complete all terms of the deal."

"We don't have that," my wife says suddenly. "Where am I supposed to get that kind of money?"

The prosecuting attorney shakes her head. "You decided to take money from the people of Brighton Falls, Mrs. Dixon. No one held a gun to your head and forced you to do it. Where you get the restitution is up to you, but I would suggest that you carefully consider this offer. There will be no other."

My skin tingles as I shake my head. "What about the other one hundred fifty thousand you claim she stole?"

"I have made no such claim, Mr. Dixon," Ms. Wood replies. "What I have said is that there is two hundred thousand missing from the accounts she managed, of which I surmise that your wife is directly responsible for around fifty thousand dollars. She will be asked to make repayment of that portion of the money missing as well as to deliver important evidence against various other individuals."

"Evidence? Against who?"

"Well, the mayor, to begin with." I feel the blood run from my head to my feet as I hear the prosecuting attorney mention Craig Leighton. This is not good, especially if he gets caught helping Tori with this case. Everything could go south very quickly.

"The mayor is involved?" I ask as I try to shield my wife at least a little from Ms. Wood's inquisition.

"I believe so, as well as two or three others." She levels her eyes at me. "You do understand that you are not allowed to speak with anyone outside this room concerning what is said in here today, correct?"

I nod my head. "Mr. Millhouse has already made us aware."

"Has he?" She smiles over at our attorney. "Has he also made you aware that if your wife refuses to aid this investigation, I could potentially bring charges against her for the full amount we believe to be missing from the accounts? A prison sentence for several felonies in the commission of a variety of crimes related to this could send her away for twenty or more years. Would the two of you like to see Mrs. Dixon spend the next two decades in lockup?" There is a coldness in the prosecutor's eyes as she watches our reactions. She means business, and I can't see how Mr. Millhouse can shield us any longer from cooperating.

"We will consult, Ms. Wood," he tells her as he looks over at my wife. "We need three days to figure out what we will do."

"Three days," she says as she shakes her head. "Fine, I'll allow you that. Just keep in mind that I'm not going to extend this offer one day beyond, Mr. Millhouse. Either you convince Mrs. Dixon to give testimony against her coworkers and others in city government, or I will be forced to hang anything and everything I have on your client. The choice is hers." Ms. Wood stands from her seat and her two companions do the same. They leave the room and at this point we are alone.

"Should I?"

"We won't discuss this here," Mr. Millhouse says. "Never talk out something like this in the room used by your prosecutor, Mrs. Dixon."

"This isn't a game," I say gruffly.

"No, it isn't," he admits. "However, it becomes a game to the prosecution. She will use whatever she has to try to taint your wife's image and then she will try to influence a jury to believe that whether she has enough proof or not, Mrs. Dixon is guilty. Trust me, we do not need to speak in this room about what we can do or what we will do. We should go back to my office and have a real heart-to-heart."

"Agreed," Tori replies. "Let's go." She stands up, and I follow along with the attorney. We leave the courthouse, our minds all swimming with whatever we need to decide in the next three days. This will not be an easy decision, but Tori's life hangs in the balance. Whatever is done, it will need to be in her best interests.

Chapter Nine: Only So Much

I have just completed an important furniture sale as Mayor Leighton walks into my store. "Can you spare a moment?" he asks as he walks right up to me.

"I nod in the direction of the buyers before I quietly say to Craig, "I have to finish this up first, but if you want to come back later..."

"We need to talk *now,* Andy. This is really important." I watch as the man turns and looks toward the door he just walked through, as if he expects something to happen soon.

"Fine, just wait in my office, okay?" I point toward the door at one end of the gallery. He nods and walks away, closing the door behind him before he has a seat. Watching him through the window closely, I continue to write up the purchase for the young couple who has just bought a new bedroom suite. For fifteen minutes, Craig Leighton simply sits in the chair in front of my desk, doing nothing more than staring at the wall. He doesn't move the entire time, his attention on me every so often as he waits patiently for me to finish my work. I'm not about to hurry anything right now since I need this purchase so badly. It has been a long time since I have seen three thousand dollars come through my store at once, so I am not about to do anything to jeopardize my good fortune.

After getting my customers taken care of, I walk back to my office and close the door behind me. Looking at the mayor, I ask, "What's on your mind, Craig?"

"What's on my mind?" he asks as he shakes his head. "So, your wife is going to turn evidence on me?"

"What? Where did you hear that?"

"The prosecuting attorney," he tells me nervously. "She says Tori will blow the lid off this thing and that I am about to go to prison for everything that has happened."

"Wait a minute, Ms. Wood told you that? We only just spoke to her yesterday. Tori refused to answer any of her questions and the prosecutor warned us we had better cooperate. That's where it stands at this time, Craig."

"So, she didn't offer to help?"

"Well, not at this point." I sit down on the end of the desk nearest my old friend. "Craig, there's nothing you have to worry about anyway, is there?"

He shivers a little as he shakes his head. "I'm going to have to resign my position as mayor of Brighton Falls, Andy. Things are getting too hairy for me in that office and I aim to get the hell out of this place as soon as I can."

"Wait, you're trying to help us, though, right? You can't just leave. We need you to help us get some of the really terrible stuff wiped out..."

"You don't understand, Andy. This woman, the prosecutor, is looking at *everything.* Any ledger that the city has is being analyzed by people with far better math skills than I have, and they are looking to hang something on me. She told me that she would make an example out of me if she must. Ms. Wood also said that Tori has promised to work with her on the case and that my name was first to come up."

"You have heard wrong," I reassure him.

The mayor rolls his eyes a little as he puts his face into his hands. "I can't help you or Tori anymore, Andy. Things are too tough now and I just want to get out of this while I still can."

I pat him on the shoulder. "We need you to keep working on getting things fixed in the books, Craig. You promised that you could cover that fifty thousand dollars. Have you done that yet?"

"Are you kidding?" he says incredulously. "That woman is looking to come after me."

"She's just bluffing her way to get to you. Ms. Wood is apparently playing all ends of this puzzle to see who cracks first." It all makes sense now as I see her game plan. Turn everyone into a potential rat and see which one flips first. Whoever gives the juiciest information wins the prize, so to speak. "That damned prosecuting attorney can't be trusted."

"Maybe so, but I think resigning would be best for me. If I no longer have anything to do with this whole mess, maybe it would then go away for me."

"That would be tantamount to admitting your guilt, Craig," I say as I get up from the end of my desk and walk over to my chair. I sit down and lean forward to rest my elbows on top of the desk. "What can we do to keep you in the mayor's office?"

"I don't know what can be done, Andy. I'm at my wit's end with this whole thing and the way the council has decided to shut me out on some of their decisions now. I'm tired and I want to just give it up."

"There has to be some way to convince you to stay." I look at the receipt I just finished for the couple who bought the bedroom suite. "I have three thousand on me right now, if that would help. Would that give you some incentive to stick around? If you need more, I could wire more into your bank in the next week or so."

"No," Mayor Leighton says as she shakes his head. "I am pretty certain they are watching my account. The prosecutor mentioned some things that causes me to feel a bit wary about what she might see pass through there."

"Oh," I reply. "Then what? Cash?"

"Even that could be dangerous, Andy." He thinks for a minute, a strange look coming over his face after a short while. "I enjoyed my time with Tori the other day, you know. Do you think she would be willing to carry things a bit further with me?" Craig smiles as he asks the question. "Sticking around for that would be worth the risk to me. I won't ask for any money and your wife will have my assurance that I can do my best to keep the top on this thing."

I take a deep, steady breath as I think about the offer. Just a few weeks ago, I would have torn a man's head from his shoulders for suggesting that Tori have sex with him. However, in light of the fact that she has already given him a blow job in his office and that she is in deep trouble, I can see where we might be able to come to a deal. "I would need to talk to her about that, Craig," I tell him as look out the office window into the furniture sales floor. "If Tori is up to it, I guess I couldn't say no. How much further do you want to go?"

Craig clears his throat. "Well, I would like to have the full experience, if that would be something that the two of you would be amenable to."

"You mean full sex, right?" I watch him nod, a line of goosebumps suddenly running along my back and neck. "That's a steep price, you know."

"It's not that steep," he argues. "There are lots of women in this town right now who make all kinds of deals with others for what they need."

"Some think that Tori runs a brothel. She has been accused of being paid for sex on several occasions, and I can tell you that this is something she is very sensitive about. Could you keep this all secret if she were to agree to have sex with you?" I get hard thinking about the mayor having sex with my wife. My petite wife would make a fine fuck for the mayor if Tori is willing to give in to his proposal. "I would have to be there, to ensure that everything worked out okay."

"You want to watch?" Craig asks with a grimace.

"Yes," I reply. "Tori might accept this if I ask her in the right way. Trying to keep me out of it will not help convince her to do it."

"This is for her, though."

"My wife still has common sense, Craig. I have to be with her when it happens."

Though he is somewhat resistant to the idea, Mayor Leighton finally relents, saying, "Okay, I think I can live with that. Where would it happen?"

"Not at home," I say as I look over at him. "People are watching to see what happens between all of the people on the prosecuting attorney's list. We can't afford having any sort of record that ties the two of you together at the same time. The woman will use that against us all."

"Agreed," he replies. "Not at my home either, for the same reason. What about leaving the county and finding a hotel?"

I shake my head. "Tori is barred from leaving the county until the court allows for it." Suddenly, I get an idea. "The bed and breakfast in Dawson," I say with a smile. "They won't know any of us there and we can show up at separate times."

"That's a nice place, from what I hear," the mayor says. "I wouldn't mind that location."

"I'll have to run that by my wife, though."

"I'm going to book a room today," Craig replies. "Get her there this weekend. On Saturday, if that would work."

I nod my head. "I'll have to get her to okay this, though."

"Just bring her," he replies. "Bring her and we will talk to her together. Maybe Tori will give in easier if she gets the full picture." Craig thinks a moment before adding, "I will do everything I can for her, Andy. I promise you that, so long as I get what I want in return."

"I understand," I tell him. "I'll have her there Saturday afternoon." The mayor gets up from his chair and goes to my office door, opening it and leaving as quickly as he came in. "Shit," I say under my breath as I think about my wife and how I am going to convince her to leave the house on Saturday. Whatever I do, I have to get her to agree to fuck Craig Leighton. Nothing less will be acceptable for him.

Chapter Ten: A Rude Awakening

"I can't believe you did that," my wife says as she shakes her head and paces around after I have revealed the real reason we are at the bed and breakfast in Dawson. "You said this was a getaway just for the two of us, Andy. You fucking lied to me!"

"Honey, I'm sorry. I didn't really lie, though. I just didn't give you the full truth of the matter for why we were coming here."

"Fuck!" Tori turns her dark eyes in my direction. For such a small woman, she has a commanding presence when she is angry, causing my skin to prickle as she almost shrieks, "I am not going to live up to that damned rumor that keeps going around, Andrew! I fucking hate the fact that everyone is talking about me the way they are. Why do you feed into this?"

I put a hand up as I try to calm her down. "Tori, this is important. If Craig decides to go ahead and resign his position as mayor, someone else will be appointed by the city council to finish out his term. You know the council believes you are guilty of everything the prosecuting attorney has been investigating. The current mayor is the only one right now keeping everything together."

"Fuck!" she exclaims for a second time as she begins to pace the small room.

"You need to keep it down, Tori. There are other people staying here. We don't need to draw attention to us right now."

"Why not?" my wife asks indignantly. "You're going to feed into the fucking rumor by paying off the mayor with my body."

"Dammit, honey." I shake my fists at the side of my body as I become angry. "Why are you making this so difficult? You already sucked the guy off and I figured you would be fine with taking things just a bit further. What the hell is the problem in letting him have a little more fun?"

Her eyes narrow as she says to me, "You are actually enjoying this, aren't you?"

"What? Don't be ridiculous, Tori."

"You are fucking looking forward to watching Mayor Leighton have sex with me. I can see it in your eyes, you piece of shit."

"Sweetheart, I am only doing this to help you stay out of prison, remember? This has nothing to do with any sort of fantasy you think I might have in mind." Tori shakes her head. She doesn't believe me, and to be honest, there is a bit of truth to what she says. I do look forward to seeing Craig fuck my wife. It's a strange thing that has grown inside me since the first day this whole sex-for-favors thing got started when Tori gave the mayor a blow job. That was completely unexpected on my end, but the effects of it were considerable as I thought hard about how much enjoyment I gleaned from that day's activity.

"Whatever," Tori says as she turns around after hearing a knock at the door. "I don't want to do this, Andy."

"Just hear him out, okay?" I walk over to the door and open it to allow Mayor Leighton into the room.

"Glad to see the two of you found this little nugget in Dawson." Craig smiles as he closes the door.

"Why here?" Tori asks. "It's not as if Dawson is so far away from Brighton Falls. It's only a half-hour drive. People here could know any one of us."

"The people who work at this bed and breakfast are good friends of mine, Tori. They know how to keep a secret." I suddenly get the feeling that this is not the first time our town's mayor has made use of this location. Have there been other women who needed favors of Brighton Fall's highest elected official? I would not be surprised if I were to discover that to be the case.

"She's nervous," I say to him.

"Nervous?" Craig smiles at Tori for a moment before saying, "I have promised your husband that for this small favor I will continue fighting for you, Tori. This has not been easy, so Andy and I have talked it over and this seems to be a fair trade."

"I'm not a fucking object or some animal on the farm with which to be bartered, Craig. This doesn't sit well with me when I think about all the people who are already accusing me of being a paid whore."

"Well, you're not getting any actual money for this, right?" Though he obviously means it as a joke of sorts, I cringe as I see my wife's reaction.

"I'm not a fucking *whore!"* Tori crosses her arms and sits down on a chair at the side of the room.

"Honey, that's not what he meant. Please, you have to do this. Otherwise, we are going to have to face the prosecuting attorney with nothing to show for it. We will lose, Tori. I don't want to lose you." My wife and I have spoken at length about the prospect of her going to prison. The threat is very real, with Ms. Wood ready to do all she can to throw Tori behind bars for as long as she can. This is almost a game to her as she goes through all the characters in the true-life play, twisting and turning words as she narrows her focus upon my wife. The prosecuting attorney is fanatical in her attempts to finger Tori with every one of the crimes she believes have occurred, and I can't stand the thought of losing the love of my life for a decade or more.

Tori takes a deep breath as she pulls some hair from her face with a hand. "I don't know what to do."

"I think that part is simple," the mayor tells her. "Just strip down and lie back. I'll do all the work if you would like."

My wife's dark eyes look up at him with a measure of contempt as she considers the only real option she has left. Quietly standing to her feet, Tori begins to unbutton her blouse, which prompts Craig to begin to remove his own clothes. "I guess that's her answer," I say quietly as I move to one side of the room to watch the two of them together.

As Tori's bra comes off, her small, firm breasts cause me to smile a little, her puffy nipples hard in the cool air of the room. My wife's skin is softer than most, given such careful treatment with bath oils and lotions every day to the point of obsession. She likes soft skin, as do I, so I am so thankful for the way Tori attends to this physical attribute.

Next, she pulls down her blue jeans along with the small pair of thong underwear she is wearing. I feel my cock become hard as her smooth, waxed muff is now easily seen by the mayor. This is the first time he has seen her breasts or her pussy, so the erection he gets just before he pulls off his own pants and underwear is complete. Arousal takes no time at all for the mayor as he looks over my wife's sexy body.

"Damn, you are a hot little thing, aren't you?" he says to her as he walks up to my small wife. At five-two and one hundred pounds, Tori is a true spinner. There have been many times during sex that I have simply lifted her up and put her on my cock, fucking her while standing next to a bed. The act of holding her like that turns me on completely, causing me to come so quickly that Tori then has to ask me to finish her off. I'm selfish that way sometimes, I suppose, but when I am so close to an orgasm I really don't give much thought to the other person I am fucking.

"Let's get this over with," Tori says as she lies back on the bed, her legs opening enough that her little pecan opens up for Mayor Leighton to get a nice view of her clitoris.

"Yes, ma'am," he replies as he moves toward her, his dick waggling side to side with each step.

Craig bends over to kiss my wife, but she turns her face from him. "No, I don't want that. Just do what you want to do and let's move on."

"Okay," he says as he looks over at me. I shrug my shoulders and shake my head as I feel my own cock becoming hard. "Can I do this, then?" The mayor puts a hand on Tori's small breast, squeezing it gently as he rolls her nipple around between his fingers. "Wow, this is so firm and perky."

He reaches down toward my wife's other breast and does the same, both of his hands now fondling Tori's chest. "Shit," I say under my breath as I watch him play with her nipples. “How does that feel, honey?” I ask her.

“Fuck off,” she tells me as she tries to ignore what the man is doing to her. It’s obvious, though, that he is having an effect on her as her nipples become hard.

“Your skin is so soft, Tori,” Craig tells her as he runs his hands along her stomach and legs. “You have got to be softer than any other woman I have ever been with.” The mayor bends down and takes a nipple into his mouth, sucking on it as a hand runs along Tori’s leg. My wife closes her eyes as he does this, biting her lip just a little as she tries to ignore the man fondling her.

I walk over to the side of the bed so that I can watch better. Pulling a chair from the side, I have a seat and watch as the man next to my wife moves from one nipple to the other to lick and play with her. “She likes that.”

Craig lifts his head. “I thought she might. She doesn’t like to say much, does she?”

“Fuck you,” Tori growls as she keeps her eyes closed.

“Okay.” The mayor chuckles a little as he begins to kiss down toward my wife’s soft pussy. She doesn’t resist him as he gently pushes her legs to either side, inhaling her aroma with a smile on his face. “You smell nice.”

Tori opens her eyes to stare down at the man. “I didn’t get a chance to shower today. It serves you right.”

“No, I wasn’t joking,” he tells her. “I love it when a woman smells like a woman and not some bath soap.” Craig kisses her just above her slit, then moves into Tori’s valley.

“Fuck,” my wife says as her feet point a little. “Dammit, Craig.”

The mayor lifts his head and says to her, “You like that, huh? Well, you taste wonderful, Tori. I’m going to make sure that I get my tongue everywhere I can down here.” Mayor Leighton goes back down on my wife and begins to kiss, lick, and nip at every part of her sweet vulva.

"Dammit," she groans as her hands go down to his head. Tori puts her fingers into Craig's hair as he eats her out. "Holy fuck, what are you doing to me?" My wife loves oral sex, though I would have thought that as resistant as she was to the idea of fucking the mayor she would have simply not allowed herself to become so aroused. As he gives her pleasure, Tori becomes wet and begins to grind into his face.

"Oh, honey," I moan as I open up my own pants. I pull my hard cock from inside and begin to play with it as I watch Tori pull Craig's face hard into her snatch. "Do you like this, Tori?"

She begins to breathe hard as her face turns a little red. Looking at me, Tori replies, "Fuck you, dammit. I wasn't supposed to like this. Holy shit, I wasn't supposed to like this." Tori closes her eyes as he continues to lick at her warm, wet muff.

The mayor looks up at her and asks, "Do you want me to stop?"

"Fuck you," she tells him as she pulls on his head to force him back into her wet slit. The answer Tori gives him, while still verbally resistant, causes me to begin to feel as if I might shoot my load across the bed at the couple. I stop myself and wait as I watch the two lovers continue to enjoy their time together.

"Oh, this shouldn't be happening," Tori suddenly says after another minute of oral from Craig. "Oh, fuck...*nahhh...UHHHH!!!*" She pulls hard on his head while arching her back and grinding into the mayor's face. *"Ohhh...ohhh..."* Tori lets out a series of near-squeaks as she comes hard with his face buried in her crotch. I want to come now, but I don't. I want to be patient as I think about how much more Mayor Leighton will want from my wife. *"Shit...stop..."* Tori pushes his face out of her muff as she turns to her side.

"You liked that, huh?" Craig laughs as he pulls her back to her back. "My turn, sweetie."

"Wait," she says to him breathlessly. "A condom. You have a condom, right?"

"Nope," he tells her as he pushes his cock against her wet labia. "I want to go bareback, Tori." The mayor looks at me. "Would you be okay with that?"

"I'm fine with it," I say immediately. "I don't have a condom on me either, but this is up to Tori whether she wants to chance it."

"I'm ovulating," she says as she looks at me. "He could get me pregnant."

"You should be on the pill," I reply. For years Tori took birth control pills, but she stopped after we discovered that my sperm count is low anyway. After her time with the police chief, I suggested that she should consider getting back on the pill, but Tori insisted that there would not be another incident like that one. Well, here we are again, no condoms, and a horny man on top of her.

"Can I do this or not?" Craig asks with some frustration. My wife nods nervously at him and he begins to push his hard cock into her wet muff. "Fuck, you're so damned tight!" His beefy phallus pushes in slowly as the mayor pushes my wife's legs back.

"Just pull out when you get ready to come, okay?" She grimaces as the man does not answer her immediately. "Oh, fuck, *easy!"* Tori tries to push her legs down, but Craig continues to push them back and out, making her vagina shorter and lifting her cervix to meet the large head of his long cock. "Shit, you're too fucking long!" My wife squirms beneath her lover as he finds her cervix and pushes hard against it.

"Shit, this is nice." I watch as the mayor's abdominal muscles undulate, his torso moving slowly forward and back, pushing his long cock all the way into my wife's wet hole. His balls now tapping on my wife's dark asshole, Craig says, "I am going to come inside of you, okay?"

"No," Tori moans as she begins to grind her ass underneath the mayor. "I could get pregnant."

"I hope you do," he tells her as he bends down and kisses her on the lips, something that my wife avoided a bit earlier. To my surprise,

Tori doesn't resist him, but begins to move her tongue in and out of his mouth as she tastes him back.

"Fuck," I moan as I pre-come into my hand a little while stroking my hard manhood. The way Craig is pumping in and out of Tori's tight hole makes me want to come right now, but I struggle to hold back the urge as I enjoy seeing the two of them together.

"Oh, not again," Tori groans as her feet point into the air as they sit on the mayor's shoulders. "Fuck, it's going to happen again. Shit...*ahhhh!!!*" My wife claws at the man's back as she orgasms with him again, this time her body twisting as Craig's cock works in and out of her pussy. *"Ohhhh..."*

"I hope I get you pregnant, Tori. Shit, I...*mmmmm!!!*" The mayor pushes his long phallus deep into my wife as he begins to shoot his hot load into her tight snapper. *"Fuck...oh, FUCK!!!"* The bed shakes hard as his balls slam into Tori's asshole, his white man sauce launching deep inside her womb. If he has very many sperm cells at all, Craig is likely to father a child with my wife.

"Oh, shit..." I begin to spurt into the air as I think of him getting Tori pregnant. *"Dammit!"* Some of my jism lands on the bed near my wife as I continue to pump up and down on my manhood. The sex in the room is loud enough that I worry that others in the small bed and breakfast will complain, but I don't care. We are all getting something that we want out of this time today and that's all that matters to any one of the three of us. This is, after all, a sort of business arrangement.

"That was fucking awesome," the mayor says as he finally pulls out of my wife, his white semen slowly oozing from her hole. Tori says nothing, but looks at me with a stunned look on her face once she has noticed that I have come as well. "You got a bit too close to me with that," Craig says with a chuckle.

"Yeah, I was aiming for my wife." We both laugh a little as we watch Tori get up from the bed.

Reaching down for her clothes, she says to us, “I’ll be in the bathroom.” Tori goes into the small bathroom and closes the door behind her.

“Well?” I say to the mayor. “Will you be staying on and helping us with this problem Tori has?”

He nods his head. “I think I can slip that money in and then I will work on getting the paperwork fixed for everything. I know a guy.”

“A guy?” I say with a contorted look on my face.

“Yeah, that’s all you need to know,” he says with a chuckle as he puts his clothes on. “This guy knows finances better than most and he has a way to make it look like it was just a misplaced banking error. I think this will solve the problem.” He steps over to me, the smell of my wife’s pussy all over him, and adds, “There will still be the issue of the fifty thousand dollars, though. That is coming out of my own pocket and I’m having a hell of a time moving it around without the prosecutor knowing about it. I would expect that I would eventually get that money back.”

“You will,” I promise. “It might take a while, but I’ll work on it.”

“That will work,” Craig tells me with a smile. “Anyway, feel free to stay in the room for the night. It’s rented until morning anyway.” He smiles as he slips his shoes on before getting up and opening the door to the room. Soon the mayor is gone while Tori is still in the bathroom. I simply sit and wait, hopeful that the guy that Craig knows will be able to help clear this thing up.

Chapter Eleven: A Hard Bargain

I answer a knock at our front door and let the attorney we have hired, Thomas Millhouse, to come inside. "Thanks for seeing me," he says as he walks past me and into our home.

"Well, you sounded pretty eager to talk to us when you called. Please, have a seat." I wait for the young attorney to sit down before going back to the bedroom to get Tori.

"Hello, Mr. Millhouse," she says as she comes into the living room. She reaches out and shakes the young man's hand before we both sit down on the sofa nearby.

Nodding his head, he asks, "So, how have things been for the two of you over the past couple of weeks since we met with the prosecuting attorney? Have there been any messages from her or from her office?"

I look over at my wife before answering, "We haven't heard from her since the deposition."

"Good," he says with a smile that seems a little too nervous for my liking. Taking a breath, he then asks, "Have you kept yourselves busy with things other than meeting up with other people involved in the money issues at city hall?"

"Um, yeah," Tori says as she looks hard into the man's eyes. "We are keeping away from everybody and just trying to make whatever money we can at the furniture store."

"So, no visits to any councilmembers or to the mayor's house?"

"No," I say before asking, "What's this about, Mr. Millhouse. Is something bothering you?" I'm not one on beating around the bush when it comes to matters of importance, especially when those matters could mean a long jail term for Tori.

He clears his throat as he clasps his hands together on his lap. "Ms. Wood contacted me this morning. She says that she has a witness that can place the two of you at a bed and breakfast in Dawson three days ago."

I shrug my shoulders. "So, what? We stayed in the county, Mr. Millhouse. Can't Tori and I have a little relaxation when things get so damned stressful?" My heart thumps as I think about why we were there. Could it be that the prosecuting attorney had us followed and spied upon?

"What you are doing is dangerous," he says flatly as he looks from me to my wife. "There is a person who is willing to testify under oath that not only did you go to the bed and breakfast, but that Mayor Leighton was at the same bed and breakfast that day for about two hours." He leans forward and asks Tori, "Do I need to know something about this little excursion, Mrs. Dixon? I am your attorney, after all, and I won't share privileged information with the prosecution. However, I can't promise and adequate defense if I am to be blindsided with bits of information like this."

"She's fucking following us around?" Tori says as her face turns red. "What sort of person follows people around?"

"The sort that want to get a criminal conviction, Mrs. Dixon," the attorney replies matter-of-factly. "Ms. Wood is a determined professional, and this means a lot to her and to the promises she has made to clean up corruption in the county. This case is the lynchpin in her entire prosecutorial plan."

"Why me?" Tori sobs a little. "Why does she want to ruin me?"

Mr. Millhouse sighs before answering my wife, "Ms. Wood honestly does not see this as personal. She sees it as a way to work her way up to a judgeship eventually, Mrs. Dixon. If she is able to get several high-profile convictions around the county, she would be well placed for nomination to a position at either a state or federal court. This is the ultimate goal of any prosecutor. This is her endgame." He looks over at me and asks, "You do understand that if the two of you continue to see people who are on the witness list or who could be on the prosecuting attorney's list of suspects, you could both be considered conspirators and charged as such, don't you?"

"Conspirators?" I take a sudden, deep breath as I think about the possibility of having yet another charge added to my wife as well as one finally being plied against me. "We are not involved in any conspiracy," I lie.

"Well, that's not the way Ms. Wood sees it right now," he retorts as he wipes his head with his hand.

"Why are you so unsteady?" I ask him as I see his hands tremble. "Are you alright?"

The young attorney sits back in his seat as he looks over at me. "Can I get a glass of water or something to drink, please? I am not feeling all that well."

"I'll get you something," my wife tells him as she gets up from beside me. I watch Tori go into the kitchen as she wipes a tear from her face, just before she gets a water bottle from the refrigerator.

"I don't know what's going on," I say quietly to the attorney, "But you need to come clean with us about what is bothering you. It's obvious that something is seriously wrong." He nods his head as Tori comes back into the living room with the water. The attorney takes a sip before turning his attention back to us.

"This is going to sound difficult," he says as he wipes his forehead for a second time. "There is a video."

"A video?" I shake my head as I lean forward in my own seat. "What video?"

"A video from the room you stayed in while in Dawson, Mr. Dixon. A very seedy sort of video."

"Seedy?" My wife's face becomes flushed as she looks at me. "Oh, no, that's not possible. There is no way that something like that could exist. Andy and I were the only ones in the room most of the time."

"Most of the time," Mr. Millhouse parrots. "Unfortunately, the bulk of the video appears to cover the time in which a third individual was inside the room."

My mind begins to work as I think of what could be on the video, but then it dawns on me. "Do you have that video?" Mr. Millhouse nods his head. "What does it show?"

He clears his throat. "It shows Mrs. Dixon and the mayor of Brighton Falls engaged in sexual intercourse." The attorney looks at me. "It also shows that you were involved to the side of the room in an act of masturbation."

"Motherfucker," I growl as I clench my fists. "Where did that video come from?" I ask the young attorney.

"Ms. Wood received the video confidentially last night. Another person involved in the whole mess with city hall is trying to parlay the video into a deal with the prosecutor's office."

"Craig," I say as I shake my head. "That son-of-a-bitch used us to make a deal."

"That is entirely possible," he replies. "Ms. Wood believes that he might be responsible for more than one hundred thousand dollars of the missing money at city hall. He is desperate to get out of the charges, I am certain." Mr. Millhouse looks at Tori as she cries quietly. "This is a gamechanger, Mrs. Dixon. I don't know how we get through this except to go along with the prosecuting attorney's offer and hope for the best."

"Offer? You mean the one from before?" I take Tori's hand to give her a bit of comfort as I wait for the reply.

Mr. Millhouse shakes his head. "This is not the same offer, you must understand," he tells us. "Ms. Wood is asking something that I cannot advise in favor of. You must make your own decision, though."

"What does she want?" Tori asks.

After a moment of silence, the attorney replies, "She wants to have a private off-the-record meeting with the two of you in her office on Saturday afternoon. No camera, no phones, and no other people present."

"Not even our attorney?"

"Not even me, Mr. Dixon. Ms. Wood was adamant that this would be a private meeting and that you would discuss with her options for coming to some sort of resolution on this whole matter." He scoots forward in his chair so that he is much closer to me as he adds, "If you decide to do this, do not sign anything, do not admit to anything, and do not agree verbally to anything. Even though this is supposed to be completely confidential and with good intentions, I can see where it could become a real problem for us in court. This has to be a fair meeting, and I'm not sure we have any real guarantee of that." The young attorney clears his throat and adds, "If you do this, I won't be able to help you. Just be careful."

I nod my head as I look over at Tori. "What do you think of all this, honey? What do you want to do?"

She shrugs her shoulders as she looks over at Mr. Millhouse. "So, you can't be there?" He shakes his head. "That doesn't sound legal."

"It's perfectly legal for her to make the offer to meet with you like this, Mrs. Dixon. However, it is a bit outside of legal precedence for her to not include my presence in this request. When I asked her about it, she told me that this was only so that she could get a feeling for your mood toward whether you are willing to settle in some way. My guess is that she didn't like the way I interfered with her questioning at the deposition."

"But, can she use whatever we say in court against us?"

"Not directly," the attorney answers me. "However, she could take something that you say and use it to uncover other evidence."

"Even if she does uncover other evidence, that tape already has us in trouble for so-called conspiracy."

"It does," he admits. "I'm not sure she could get it admitted into court because of the way it was obtained, but there is a chance that she might find some loophole to convince the judge to grant the motion to enter it into evidence. That recording would put this whole thing underwater, Mr. Dixon. There's not much I can do to fix this now." Now I understand why Mr. Millhouse seems so nervous and concerned. He is out of his league with the case now, and he knows it.

Ms. Wood is far more experienced, and with what she knows about us now she will trounce us in court.

"So, we meet with her," Tori says resolutely. "We just go in on Saturday afternoon and throw ourselves at her mercy."

"Admit nothing," Mr. Millhouse reiterates. "She has the video, but there is a chance it can't be put into evidence."

"But there is also a chance that it could be," I remind him. "We are fucked either way."

"We meet with her." Tori looks at me before saying to the attorney, "Call her and tell her we will come to her office if she will provide you with a written promise that she won't use whatever is said in her office against me."

"Promises on paper are sometimes easily tossed by a court," Mr. Millhouse replies. "You have to be careful what you say to her. Just sit and listen."

"Fine, I'll listen," Tori replies as she wipes the tears from her eyes. "Maybe this won't be so bad."

"Maybe," I concur. "I just don't like it."

"Nor do I." Mr. Millhouse stands to his feet. "I'll make the call and request a written guarantee from her. Then I will call you and let you know the exact time for that afternoon." As my wife and I both stand to our feet as well, the attorney leans toward Tori and takes her hand to say, "I really wish you had told me about the mayor and had not met with him. From what I saw on the video, that was all about trying to help yourself out. He set you up, though, and now I'm afraid that the prosecuting attorney could use that information against you. I really think I could have helped if you had just been honest with me." Mr. Millhouse shakes his head and turns toward our door. He lets himself out as my wife and I stand silently for a moment in our living room.

"I have a bad feeling about this, honey."

"I know you do," she replies. "There's just nothing else for us to do. Craig double-crossed us to save his own ass, Andy." Tori looks at me an adds, “Please don’t ever ask me to fuck another guy again.” My wife walks out of the living room and goes back to the bedroom, closing the door again as she has done so many times since this whole mess has erupted.

“Fuck you, Craig,” I say as I pull my phone from my pocket. Then it occurs to me, “I can’t even call you to tell you want a prick you are, can I?” Any further contact with him would be evidence that there is some sort of conspiracy going on between us. “That’s probably what you are going to tell us on Saturday, isn’t it, Ms. Wood?” I say into the empty living room. “You are going to get us into your office alone so that you can gloat and bully us into sharing more information with you. By the time this whole thing is over, you will have destroyed our lives and made a name for yourself. What a big girl you are.” The snarky remark to myself gives me a brief smile before a scowl returns to my face. We will now have to deal with Ms. Wood, no matter the cost.

Chapter Twelve: A Better Deal

We get to the prosecuting attorney's office on the other side of town just before three o'clock, the time Patricia Wood instructed our attorney that we should arrive. We walk into the large building and make our way to the third floor where she is waiting for us. As we do, I notice how strange it is to be inside a public building on a weekend like this. "No one is here, but the door is open," I say to Tori. "I guess she left it open for us?"

"She must have," my wife agrees. Turning to me and taking my arm into her hands, Tori stops me to add, "Andy, I'm really worried about this. Are you sure we should go in there without Mr. Millhouse present?"

I look down at my wife as I try to manage a soft smile. "You made the decision to do this, remember? We have to follow through and at least listen to what Ms. Wood has to say."

"She's going to try to ruin me, Andy. She's going to ruin *us*."

"Maybe," I reply. "But keep in mind that the prosecuting attorney wants to see us for some reason. There is a chance that this whole case isn't as open and shut as what we might have thought. Maybe she wants to cut a deal with us like she did with the mayor."

Tori's countenance changes. "I want to kill that asshole for setting us up with that video."

I tap my wife on the arm as I reply, "Don't say that sort of thing around here, honey. We don't need the prosecutor to go after us for making threats against Craig." She nods as we continue to walk toward the prosecutor's office again.

Knocking three times on the door, my wife and I wait for a response from the other side. The door slowly opens, and we see Patricia Wood on the other side. "Welcome to my office, Mr. and Mrs. Dixon. Please come inside." We walk quietly past her as she closes the door behind us, my nerves now completely on edge as I would assume are my wife's. "Can I get the two of you anything to drink? Some water or a soft drink?" She smiles in a strange, sickly-sweet way toward the two of us as she waits patiently for an answer.

"Water," Tori finally says as she looks up at me. I nod my head to let the prosecuting attorney know that I will accept some water as well before we have a seat at a long table in the office.

"I'm sorry about causing you to have to get out on a Saturday, but my schedule has been very tight lately." Ms. Wood smiles again as she hands us each a bottle of water. I open the top of my bottle and take a quick sip as I study the way the prosecuting attorney looks today. She is not wearing her normal professional attire, but instead she has her shoulder-length blonde hair pulled back into a ponytail and only a touch of makeup on her face. Her clothes include a light blue tee shirt as well as a pair of grey sweatpants and tennis shoes. This is a far cry from the sort of look Ms. Wood attempts to put forth on a regular work day or in court. It surprises me a little that she looks more like a girl-next-door type of woman than what I would have expected to be possible with her. There is an attractive quality to her that I have not seen before, and it turns me on just a little.

"So, what is this all about?" I ask as Tori and I look across the table at the prosecuting attorney.

She clears her throat and takes a drink out of her own water bottle. "I'm sure Mr. Millhouse has explained to you that I have come across an important video concerning the two of you and Mayor Leighton, correct?"

"Yes," I reply. "However, I'm not sure that you simply came across it. I would suspect that someone recorded it without our permission and then handed it over to you."

The prosecuting attorney nods her head. "Well, I guess you are right in that respect. It is a video that was produced in a way that a court might find to be less than savory."

"But is it legal?" Tori chimes in. "We didn't give permission for the video. Hasn't the mayor violated some law by not telling us that he was doing that?"

"Possibly," she admits. "However, that could get to be a bit sticky if he were to ever be charged." Ms. Wood smiles briefly before adding, "I don't see Mr. Leighton being charged in the near future, though."

"The video is illegal, though." I want to nail her down saying it, but I can see that she is sharper than most attorneys.

"Possibly," she says again. "However, if you are questioning whether it is admissible in court in a case such as the one that I will probably bring against the both of you, I would have to say that it probably is admissible. It would entirely depend on the judge, of course, so it's a crap-shoot for everyone involved. If I take it to court and try to win a conviction against either of you, the judge could throw it out or the jury could look very unkindly to the way it was obtained. However, it could go the other way and lead to at least two convictions." Her blue eyes focus heavily on the two of us as she asked, "Are you a gambling sort of people? Or would you prefer to bet on a sure thing?"

"What are you talking about?" I ask as I feel a twinge of anger rising inside me. I don't like to be toyed with, and this certainly feels as if Tori and I are being toyed with by the prosecuting attorney.

"I'm talking about considering whether I up the charges against the two of you to present to the court."

"What charges?" Tori shakes a little as she squeezes my hands tightly.

"Well, there are the charges of money laundering, public funds embezzlement, and failure in public fiduciary responsibilities. These are all three financial felonies and each one is a two-to-five-year sentence if you are convicted."

"Shit," I say as I shake my head. "Please don't do that to her."

"To *her?*" the prosecutor says to me as she smiles. "It gets better, Mr. Dixon. I can add a State charge of conspiracy to taint a witness, conspiracy to commit bank fraud, and conspiracy to give false information to an officer of the court. Those charges would be against both of you, and with those you are both looking at the potential of never seeing the light of day outside of a prison again." Her eyes are sharp as she looks from one to the other of us. "This would be the end of everything you have worked so hard for in your life together. The court would most likely turn your store into a State asset to be auctioned for any fines stemming from a guilty verdict and then your home would be lost." Patricia Wood takes a quick breath before adding, "The two of you would never see each other again since the two prisons you would be sent to are at opposite ends of the state."

"No," I say as I feel myself begin to shake along with my wife. "Please don't do this to us. We didn't mean to do any of this, really. It has all been about some unfortunate circumstances in our life..."

"Okay, I understand that you don't have to say anything here today, but don't try to fill my ears with this bullshit, Mr. Dixon," the prosecuting attorney says as she stares back at me. "I know you were just trying to help your wife, but the fact is you have both screwed yourselves over. There's just not much I can do to help you unless you are willing to cooperate."

Tori squeezes my hand again as she asks Ms. Wood, "What do you want us to do and what is it worth to you?"

The prosecutor looks at the two of us as she smiles slightly. "I have a proposal that is a little off from what is considered a typical idea, Mrs. Dixon." She pauses a moment and asks, "May I call you Tori?" My wife nods. "Tori, I am willing to offer you a sort of workaround to the charges I have mentioned."

"A workaround? For all of them?"

The prosecutor grimaces a little before she responds, "Well, to most of them. I could see possibly only charging you for failure in public fiduciary responsibility, as a misdemeanor instead of a felony, with community service only as your sentence." She leans forward in her chair to add, "I would also expect the money to be repaid to the city."

"The money? How much?" I want to hear the actual figure from the prosecuting attorney before we agree to anything. Around two hundred thousand is missing, and I don't want us to have to be responsible for every penny of that amount.

"Fifty-two thousand, approximately," Ms. Wood replies. "I could see working out a payment plan of eight to ten years on this, but it would include additional fines and interest charges."

"I understand," Tori says with a ray of hope in her.

"What do you want?" I ask as I continue to be doubtful this is a real offer. "There's something else in this whole mess that you will expect from us. I know there is."

The prosecuting attorney nods her head. "I'm glad you understand this idea of *quid pro quo,* Andy," she says without asking whether I would be offended if she used my first name. "I do expect something in return. It is the reason the two of you are here today."

"Anything," my wife says as she looks at me and then at Ms. Wood. "Whatever you want, if you can reduce the charges and keep us out of prison, I will do it."

Ms. Wood looks at me and says, "This will mean that I won't charge you at all either, if she takes this plea deal."

"What is it?" I reply with a measure of aggravation.

The prosecuting attorney stands up and walks over to our side of the table. She sits down in a chair beside my wife and says, "I hear that you have been offering sex to other guys in order to get some cooperation from them. I want to know who they are and what you have done with them. You would also be expected to be a witness in those cases."

"But, that would incriminate me," she tells Ms. Wood.

"Not if I give you full immunity," the prosecutor replies. "Anything you say in those cases will only be used to go after the men who have tried to leverage sex or sex acts against you."

"Damn," I mumble under my breath. This will mean that not only the mayor could be charged with something, but so could the chief of police in Brighton Falls.

"Is that it?" Tori asks.

Ms. Wood shakes her head. "Not quite. I also have a personal request."

"A personal request?" Looking at my wife and then back at the prosecuting attorney, I ask her, "What sort of personal request?"

She smiles at Tori as she asks, "Why did you give the mayor a blow job?"

Shocked, my wife says, "I can't believe he told you about that."

"I think he wanted to be sure he covered all of his bases with me before he left my office a couple of weeks ago. Mayor Leighton really doesn't want to go to prison either, although I am inclined to allow him to go down for what he has done."

"Even though he gave you the video?"

"Yes," the prosecutor replies. "So, why did you do it? Why would you give a blow job to a man like him?"

"It's obvious, isn't it?" Tori says.

"Honey, please. Remember, you don't have to offer any information to her right now. We came to hear her out, and we have. We can go home and think this through, right?"

"No, Andy," my wife says to me as she looks intently at the prosecuting attorney. "Ms. Wood, I gave that man a blow job because he said he would be willing to help me if I did it. However, you can see where that has left me now."

"Holding the bag," the prosecutor replies, causing Tori to nod her head. "I won't cross you, though, Tori. I think you know you can trust me." Patricia Wood smiles as she reaches out and takes my wife's hand. "Would you be willing to give me a little oral to close this deal?"

"What the fuck?" I stand up and tap my wife on the shoulder. "Tori, let's go. She's just messing around with us now. Ms. Wood, this isn't funny, you know."

"I'm not trying to be humorous, Andy. I am offering to let a lot of things slide if your wife will eat me out right now, in this office." My cock begins to get hard and the prosecuting attorney notices it. "Besides, I think this is something you might like to see as well."

"Honey," my wife says as she looks back at the bulge in the front of my pants. I sit down to hide it as Tori turns around and looks the other woman in the eyes. "Are you serious? You would take everything down to just that one charge if I testify against the men who wanted things from me and I do the same for you that I did for them?"

"Well, you can't really suck my dick, but you could run your tongue over my clit, Tori." Ms. Wood smiles as she stands up. "Shall I take my clothes off or not?"

"Are you a lesbian?" I ask her.

"No," the prosecuting attorney says directly. "But I might be a little bisexual. I can't really be sure since I have never actually done this."

"Then why ask her for this?"

"The video," she replies. "Something about that video and listening to the mayor describe what Tori did for him has gotten me a bit wet. I want to know what it's like for Tori to put her mouth to my pussy."

"I am willing to do it," I say with a small measure of my horniness showing through.

"I thought about that at first," Ms. Wood says. "However, the more I thought about it, the more I wanted your wife to do it for me." The prosecuting attorney pulls her sweatpants down along with her thong panties, revealing a nice landing strip of hair just above her waxed pussy lips. She then pulls up on her sweatshirt to reveal that she is even smaller chested than my wife and that she is not wearing a bra at all.

"Over here," she tells my wife as she takes her hand and leads her over to a chaise lounger at the other side of the office. As the prosecutor lies back on the lounge and opens her legs, she tells Tori, "Take off your clothes, okay?"

"Honey," I say as she looks back at me. "Are you really going to do this?"

"Yeah," she replies calmly. "I'm going to do it to get myself free from this whole thing, Andy." Tori begins to work on her own clothing, stripping down to be completely nude in about a minute or so time. She then reaches back and puts her shoulder-length hair into a ponytail to keep it out of her face while she eats Ms. Wood's snatch.

"Damn," I say softly as I watch Tori bend down and begin to kiss at the prosecuting attorney's puffy labia. "I would have never thought that I would ever see you do this to another woman." Tori says nothing as she licks at the other woman's wet pussy.

"Oh, this is much better than I thought it would be," Ms. Wood moans as I walk up to the two women. Looking up at me, she asks, "Do you like to see her do things with other people, Andy? Is this a turn-on for you?"

"A little," I admit as my wife's dark-haired head moves around in the other woman's crotch.

"Fuck, Tori is really good at this. I think she might be a little bisexual." Ms. Wood closes her eyes and bites her lip a little as she enjoys my wife's tongue-work on her twat.

"Come here," Ms. Wood says to me as she reaches out for me. I step forward and she asks, "Would you pull out your cock for me? I just want to see it while she does this."

"You've already seen it in the video," I retort. "Why would you need to see it now?"

"Please," she says to me as she puts on hand on my wife's head. I don't stop the prosecuting attorney as she works to pull down the zipper on my pants, reaching in once she does to pull out my erect penis. "Fuck, you have a big one. Help me get it out, okay?" My cock is so hard that I have to unbuckle my pants and pull everything down to get my manhood out for her.

"There," I say as I move close enough for the prosecutor to touch it.

"I don't want to get you off, I just want to hold it, okay?" She looks down at my wife and says, "Keep going, Tori. I'm getting really close." The taller woman begins to arch her back a little as she pulls hard on my cock. "Dammit, she's good."

"She's my wife. Of course, she is good."

Ms. Wood laughs. "Did you teach her everything she knows about eating a pussy, Andy?"

"Who else would have?" I laugh a little with her as she gently strokes my hard rod. "This is really driving me nuts. Are you sure I can't come?"

"No, don't come." Biting her lip again, the prosecutor asks, "Would you play with my nipples, though? I want those played with so that I can get over the top with this." She smiles at me as I reach down and begin to gently massage and pinch her light pink nipples. "Fuck, that's it. Keep it up like that. Maybe a little harder, okay?" I twist lightly as Ms. Wood moans, my wife now getting a great deal of pussy juice all over her face. "Pull my nipples a little harder, Andy. Stretch them a little." I do as she asks, pulling her nipples just hard enough that I can't imagine pulling them any further without causing her some real pain.

"Is this good?"

"Very good," she tells me. "Keep going. I'm close."

"Damn, I wish you would let me come. It wouldn't take me long, you know."

"No," she says again as she begins to breathe hard. "Fuck, I'm going to have an orgasm. It's right there." Ms. Wood swallows hard as my wife fingers her vagina while lapping at the prosecutor's wet pussy lips. "Shit...*uhhhhh...*" The tall woman heaves hard as her toes curl and her back arches hard. *"Fuuuuck!"* Gritting her teeth, Patricia Wood keeps coming as Tori licks her muff hard and fast. *"Ohhh...uhhhh..."* The woman pulls my cock hard as well while I play with her nipples. I want to come all over her, but I know she doesn't want me to do it. I'm afraid that if I do it I might ruin whatever deal Tori and I have with her.

"I'm coming...I'm sorry...*mmmm...*" Suddenly, I lose control and begin to spurt all over the prosecuting attorney's upper body, showering her breasts with my semen as she continues to pull on me. *"Ohhhh!!!"* I know she didn't want me to do this, but what can I say? There is no way that I can keep from losing my load on a beautiful woman as she plays with my cock, especially as my wife eats her out. Even though I have seen her as an evil prosecutor for the past several weeks, I can only see now how badly I wish I was the one tasting of her little lady between her legs.

My wife lifts up from between the woman's legs and wipes her face with her hands. Ms. Wood still holds my cock as she tries to squeeze the last drop of jism from it. "She told you not to come, Andy."

"It's alright," the prosecutor says as she runs a finger through a dollop of jism on her chest. Putting it to her lips, she tastes it and tells me, "You're a little salty, Andy. I like salty."

"Fuck," I reply as she finally releases my wilting penis.

The prosecuting attorney gets up from the lounge and walks up to Tori. Without asking, she takes my wife into her arms and gives her a long, wet kiss. The two women embrace for a moment, causing me to think that a second round could be forthcoming. However, Ms. Wood backs away and says, "I wanted to see what your mouth tastes like with my pussy juice all over it, Tori. Thank you."

"So, are we good?" I ask her as I tuck my cock back into my pants.

"Yes, as long as you both agree to the terms." She pushes a paper towards the two of us. It says, in dark bullet-points, exactly what she has laid out with us before. There would be a couple of men who would have additional charges laid out against them for trying to cover up the way they used my wife. "One other thing, though."

"What's that?" Tori asks as she puts on her clothes.

"You both come to my house next weekend and I return the favor." The prosecuting attorney smiles at my wife as she looks at Tori's soft pussy. "I want to taste of you next time."

My wife nods and says, "I think that would be very nice. Sure, we'll be there." My mind races as Tori signs her name and then passes the document back to me. I do the same and we get copies of everything. Leaving the public building, there is very little said between the two of us, our minds still reeling from the deal we have made.

"Crazy," I finally say as we reach the car.

"A little," Tori replies with a slightly giddy sound to her voice. "It was a little fun, too."

"I guess," I say with a smile as I feel myself get a little hard again while thinking about Ms. Wood touching my cock. "Let's just hope this all works out for us."

Sign up to my Patreon account and receive exclusive Hotwife stories every month and sexy scenes every week!

https://www.patreon.com/karlyviolet

Chapter Thirteen: His Honor

We approach the courtroom with a measure of fear and anticipation as Lori and I walk with our attorney. "I just don't get it," Mr. Millhouse says as we walk in. "I thought she would practically crucify the two of you, but now she's offering an even better plea deal than before?"

"I guess we hit it off," my wife tells him with a wide smile. "You know, she's actually very easy to talk to when you get her away from other people."

"That's just strange," he says as he looks at the sheet again. "You should have allowed me to have seen this deal before you signed it, though. That was a risky move on your part."

"It's straightforward," I tell the young attorney. "Everything is listed out and we went over it very carefully with Ms. Wood."

"But, she gets very little from this. What have you given her? A name or two that she was probably already going to prosecute to some level anyway?" Mr. Millhouse sets his briefcase on the long table in front of the judge's bench. "This is just way too easy."

"Are you worried she will screw us over?" I ask him.

He shakes his head. "She signed this with you. Though I have looked it over several times, I see nothing wrong with it. The deal is very legitimate. The only problem is going to be convincing the judge that you deserve the deal."

"The judge?" Tori sits down with us at the table. "Do you think he might reject it outright?"

"It's possible," he admits. "The judge is cut from the same cloth as Ms. Woods, so I would expect him to probably question us all pretty thoroughly about the deal. If he accepts it, that means that you will begin the community service part of it as early as next month."

"That works," Tori replies as her legs shake. "I hope he takes it."

"He will," I say as I put a hand on one of her nervous legs. "There's no reason he wouldn't."

Ms. Wood and her deputy prosecutor walk into the courtroom, their eyes only briefly meeting ours as they step to the other table to the right of ours. They too have briefcases and they open them just as the court's bailiff walks in. "All rise," he says. We all stand to our feet and look ahead at the large set waiting for the judge at his bench. "Presenting the Honorable William L. Stratton, circuit court judge."

An older man, maybe in his sixties, enters the room from a door to the side near his bench. He walks over to his seat and adjusts his black robe just a bit before sitting down. "Please be seated." We all take our seats as the judge puts on a pair of reading glasses and begins to peruse the documents in front of him. "In the case of the State versus Tori Elaine Dixon, I understand that a plea bargain arrangement has been reached?"

Ms. Wood stands up and addresses the judge. "We have an agreement."

He reads it over and asks, "Are you sure this is agreeable to the State, Ms. Wood? This is quite a reduction in charges compared to what would have been brought otherwise, correct?"

The prosecuting attorney nods her head. "Yes, Your Honor, it is a much different charge sheet that what I had originally expected to bring against Mrs. Dixon."

"May I ask why?" Judge Stratton looks over his spectacles at the prosecutor as he awaits a reasonable explanation for the reduction in charges.

"We looked into everything, Your Honor, and there just isn't enough for us to be able to convince a full jury that Mrs. Dixon was complicit in anything illegal. She made several errors on the ledgers of the city of Brighton Falls and caused about fifty thousand dollars to be misappropriated in the process, but we have been able to locate where the funds have gone, and we are consolidating them back into the account."

"So, there was no money stolen?"

"Not by Mrs. Dixon, Your Honor, but it appears there may be others involved in moving money from the city's accounts. My office is currently looking at charges against multiple other suspects."

"I see," he says as he looks over the documents before him. "This asks the Court to find that Mrs. Dixon is guilty of a misdemeanor and that she would be given one hundred hours of community service for her negligence while working as city treasurer?"

"Yes, Your Honor," Ms. Wood replies. "I think that it would be sufficient to send a message to other people working in the public trust that they must be more diligent to their duties. Mrs. Dixon was not, and it has cost her the treasurer's job and a measure of her husband's furniture business. It is my opinion there has been enough suffering over this matter."

The judge looks over at my wife and says, "Please stand, Mrs. Dixon." Tori does so as she shakes a little, knowing that the man on the bench holds her life in his hands. "Have you discussed this plea agreement in its entirety with your attorney?"

"Yes, Your Honor," she tells him.

"Do you understand that in agreeing to this, you will be admitting to a misdemeanor crime that will remain on your record for the rest of your life?"

"Yes, Your Honor," she says again.

The judge folds his hands on the top of the bench as he says, "Mrs. Dixon, it is my estimation that there is something here that I've not heard from the prosecuting attorney in the case. She tells me that there are others more responsible for what has happened, but I find that difficult to believe because you are, in fact, the former treasurer for the city of Brighton Falls. The treasurer would normally be the first one to know when money is being taken, and this idea that you accidentally misplaced one-quarter of the money missing from their accounts is somewhat laughable." The courtroom is silent as the judge looks over at the prosecutor's table for a moment. "However, there isn't much I can do to convince Ms. Wood that she should attempt to justify additional charges against you. Therefore, I am going to certify the plea agreement if you are still in favor of me doing so. Are you in favor of this, Mrs. Dixon?"

"Yes, please, Your Honor."

The older gentleman looks right at my wife as he says, "So be it. Mrs. Dixon, you are found guilty of a misdemeanor offense concerning fiduciary responsibility based upon the plea agreement brought before me this day."

"Request sentencing immediately," Ms. Wood says.

"Agreed," Mr. Millhouse states as he and I stand.

"The sentence shall be as stated in the agreement, one hundred hours of community service with no prison time to serve." Judge Stratton strikes his gavel three times after saying, "Court adjourned."

"All rise," the bailiff calls out, causing us to each stand still as the judge leaves the room.

"Finally!" Tori begins to cry a little as she hugs me tightly.

"Very nice job with your client," we hear Ms. Wood say to our attorney.

"Thank you," he replies with a smile as he shakes her hand.

"Mr. and Mrs. Dixon, I hope this resolves everything for you."

"It does," Tori says with a smile.

"Good." The prosecuting attorney begins to walk away, but turns and says to us, "Don't forget about the picnic in a couple of weeks. I expect to see you both there." The woman winks and then walks out of the courtroom with her deputy prosecuting attorney.

"What was that all about?" Mr. Millhouse asks as he looks at the two of us.

"Nothing, really," I tell him with a smile. "I think Ms. Wood wants Tori to work the picnic for some of the community service she owes. There is a lot of trash around the park when they have those, you know."

"I guess." I can tell by the way the young attorney looks at me that he is not completely convinced of the innocent nature of the invitation. "I just hope that whatever happened in that meeting with the prosecutor that everything was what it was supposed to be."

"It all worked out, didn't it? Isn't that how things were supposed to turn out?" My wife's dark eyes focus on the young attorney until he smiles a little. "Mr. Millhouse, thank you so much for your help." Tori reaches out to shake the man's hand. I do the same, and soon my wife and I are alone in the courthouse hallway.

"Well, Ms. Wood did what she promised.

"She did," Tori agrees. "But there's still a lot on my mind, honey. I want more." I'm not sure what she means by this, but I continue to walk with her to the front doors of the courthouse before we head back home for a celebratory drink of a bottle of champagne that I found for half-price a few days ago.

Chapter Fourteen: Getting Back to Normal

Things have begun to settle down for the two of us over the last few weeks since the plea agreement was accepted by the judge in court. Though we have had one phone call from Mr. Millhouse to ask how we are doing, little else about the case has had anything to do with our work or private lives. Tori, no longer the treasurer for our small town, is now working with me in my furniture store. The change in our relationship has been obvious from the first night home after the court's decision. She is a new woman and I feel a bit different as her husband. Still, there are things that need to be hashed out between us now that we have both experienced things that many married couples do not.

"So, have you thought about what we talked about the other night?" I ask her as we sit in my office after closing the store.

Tori smiles at me as she counts the day's receipts. "I've thought a little about it, Andy. Why are you asking?"

I shrug my shoulders. "Well, you know how I feel about it, right? I mean, I don't mind the thought of you having a little fun with another guy or gal once in a while."

"A gal?" she laughs. "I already let Patty eat me out, Andy. I thought that would be the end of the lesbian fetish for you." We have gotten to know the prosecuting attorney better since the court case. The two women have enjoyed a couple more sexual interludes with each other while I watched, but I could see that it was becoming a little strained on Tori's part. She isn't lesbian, and even the bisexual thing doesn't seem to be of much interest to her. Still, it caused me to have one hell of a hardon just thinking about it whenever we talked about it. I told my wife it was fine to quit her little fling with Ms. Wood, and so she did. There are no hurt feelings on either side, though. They still consider each other at the very least great acquaintances. I'm not certain that the term friends would fit the two of them, though.

"A guy or two, then," I say with a wicked grin on my face. "What do you say?"

"I don't know," Tori replies as she puts our financial ledger away in the safe. "I already have that damned reputation going around the community." Shaking her head, she asks me, "Do you think that will ever go away? Or am I just saddled with that for the rest of my life?"

"Saddled with it," I joke with her. "Look, people will talk no matter what you do. It won't matter whether it's today, tomorrow, or a decade from now, there will still be some people claiming that they personally know of someone you have fucked. I say just go along with it and laugh it off."

"That's easy for you to say," Tori chuckles as she walks up to me. I turn my chair to allow my wife to sit on my lap. "People aren't saying these things about you, Andy."

"No, they are saying that I'm the guy married to the prostitute in town." I laugh hard as she playfully slaps the top of my head.

"You're a fucking asshole, do you know that?"

"I've been told that," I say to my wife as I kiss her soft lips. I crave Tori more now than I have in a long time, probably because all her sexual energy has been channeled into other people for the past few months. Though there has been some intimacy between the two of us, my wife wants more. I thought at first that Tori wanted to be free to experiment with other women, but now I realize that she just wants to enjoy other men as I watch. That's the kink for the two of us, after all. If we fuck other people, we do it together.

"It has been a weird ride for the two of us over the past couple of months, hasn't it?" Tori reaches down and gently rubs the growing bulge in my pants. "I've done things recently that I would have never thought this time last year I would ever do." My wife finds the head of my cock through my pants and begins to toy with it.

"Yeah, I think we both have," I reply as she makes me harder. "Fuck, honey, you're going to get me going if you don't stop that."

"Oh, am I?" Tori kisses me long and hard as she embraces me, her sweet perfume filling my nostrils. She leans back after a moment and asks, "Any ideas on who I should see next?"

"For sex?" She nods her head. "Oh, hell, I don't know. Do you have someone in mind?" I can see by the look in her eyes that she definitely has someone in mind. "Who?"

Smiling, Tori replies, "I think that maybe we should see if Mr. Millhouse would be interested."

"Our attorney? *Really?"* I laugh a little as I think about the tall, muscular man who helped us navigate our legal jeopardy with the prosecutor's office. "What makes you think that he would do something like that?"

My wife looks down at me as she pushes her fingers through my shirt buttons to my bare chest. "He liked watching the video of us that Patty gave him."

"The one where Craig recorded us without our knowledge?" I say with a scowl. "How could you tell that Mr. Millhouse liked the video?"

Tori leans in close to me and whispers in my ear, "He had a bulge in his pants as he talked about it." My wife puts her tongue in my ear, causing goosebumps to rise along my neck.

"Damn, honey." I wriggle around in my seat as Tori begins to unzip my pants. It doesn't take long for her to get my hard cock out and begin to pull up on it. "Oh, fuck..."

"If he is willing to fuck me, what would you like to see him do to me, Andy?" Tori breathes lightly along my neck as she kisses me there, causing me to begin to ache for a quick orgasm.

"I don't know, Tori. What would you want him to do to you?"

She giggles before replying, "I want Thomas to start by fingering my pussy. I want to see what his well-manicured hands can do with me before anything else." Tori grinds around on top of my lap as she gently pulls on my manhood.

"And then what?"

"Then, I want him to bite my nipples." She continues to breathe lightly into my ear as she plays with me. "I want to know what it is like to have a guy gently nibble on each one until I beg him to stop."

"Dammit, sweetheart." My heart races as Tori pulls up hard on my cock, causing a drop of pre-come to ooze from the tip.

"Maybe then he can kiss down my stomach to my cunt and lick it all up. I'll be wet by then, so it would be nice if he would be willing to lap up my juices, Andy. Would you like to see him lick at my pussy?"

"Fuck, yeah," I reply almost breathlessly as I grit my teeth. "Motherfucker, Tori, you are going to make me pop soon."

"Then pop," she says with a giggle. "But, I want Thomas to pop as well. I want him to bury his cock deep inside my pussy and come inside me."

"With a condom?" I laugh.

"No condom. I want him to impregnate me, Andy." I take a quick, deep breath as I realize the game has now changed. We have now gone from simply having a nice casual fuck with someone else to *trying* to get pregnant.

"You would really want him to try to get you pregnant?"

Tori wriggles around on my lap as I get closer to coming. "You want him to fuck me when I'm ovulating, don't you? You want to know that Mr. Millhouse could get me pregnant when he fucks me without a condom."

My wife is right. I really love the kinkiness of some guy having sex with her when she could get pregnant. "I want him to fuck you while you are ovulating. We need to track that so that we can tell him when he will inseminate you."

"Inseminate," Tori whispers into my ear. "That sounds so fucking dirty, Andy."

"It *is* fucking dirty," I growl back at her. "I want Mr. Millhouse to bend you over the bed and fuck your fertile snapper until he bursts into you. Then I want you to put your ass into the air to make sure his spunk moves into your womb. Shit, I can't believe I want you to do this, but I do. I want him to get you pregnant."

"Oh, yes," Tori says as she pulls on my over and over. I can feel myself about to lose my load as she looks into my eyes. "And what happens after I'm pregnant?"

I think for a moment before replying, "Then I want you to fuck him while you get bigger and bigger. I want him to keep squirting his jism into you while you are growing with his baby." I suddenly lurch forward as I begin to spurt from my own penis. "Shit...*uhhhh!*" The first shot launches from between Tori's fingers and lands a few feet from my chair. The next is almost as far, but the third one and each one thereafter is collected by my wife's hand. *"Dammit! OHHH!!!"* I continue to come hard as I think about what it would be like to see my wife actually do this with our attorney. Thomas Millhouse would be a great choice, and I hope that she will call him later today to set something up.

"You are really messy, sweetheart," Tori says as she pulls her hand off my cock. "Any paper towels in here?"

"By the filing cabinet I tell her." I watch as she cleans off her hand and then helps me to clean myself up as well as the floor in front of the chair. After a quick tidying of the workspace, I ask Tori, "Were you serious?"

She pauses as she looks at me to ask, "Were you?"

Nodding my head, I say to my wife, "We should invite him over for dinner soon."

"Tonight," Tori chimes in quickly to my surprise, especially considering it is now six in the afternoon.

"That's pretty short notice. Why the interest in seeing him so quickly?

My wife leans over and says into my ear, "I'm ovulating sweetheart. There is an egg with his name on it. Besides, he already has the invitation for this evening." Tori smiles wickedly as she turns and leaves the office to get ready to go home.

"Wow." I sit in silence for a moment as I think about how real this new chapter is about to become. "Damn, honey. *Damn.*"

THE END

Sign up to my Patreon account and receive exclusive Hotwife stories every month and sexy scenes every week!

https://www.patreon.com/karlyviolet

Don't miss out!

Visit the website below and you can sign up to receive emails whenever Karly Violet publishes a new book. There's no charge and no obligation.

https://books2read.com/r/B-A-GIXE-ZRMKB

Connecting independent readers to independent writers.

Did you love *Hotwife Hotel Adultery - A Naughty Romance Hot Wife Novel*? Then you should read *Swingers Party - A Wife Watching Multiple Partner Hotwife Romance Novel*[1] by Karly Violet!

[2]

Five Married Couples Partake In An Unforgettable Swingers Party

Jordan's boozy night in with the lads gets a little too racy when the talk of the sexual exploits in their college years starts to drive the conversation.

Reminiscing about the multitude of women the men slept with was always going to bring out the competitive spirit in them.

And no more so as they recollect an unforgettable party where all five of the men slept with the same beautiful woman, one after the other!.

The men are older, but are still as adventurous as ever.

---

1. https://books2read.com/u/mB2Qxy
2. https://books2read.com/u/mB2Qxy

And so when a casual comment is made that all five of the married men should host a swinging party with their wives in attendance.........

..... the nervous husband mentally prepares himself as his willing wife becomes shared amongst his closest friends at the exclusive swingers party!

This scorching hot 20,000 word novel features married couple enjoying their bodies with their closest friends at an exclusive swingers party!

Read more at https://www.patreon.com/karlyviolet.

About the Author

Sign up to my mailing list to receive the two free epilogues for 'A Hotwife Adventure' and 'Hotwife Training' and to stay up to date on all of my latest releases! http://eepurl.com/c3ICWf Sign up to my Patreon account and receive exclusive Hotwife stories every month and sexy scenes every week! https://www.patreon.com/karlyviolet

Read more at https://www.patreon.com/karlyviolet.

About the Publisher

www.ingramcontent.com/pod-product-compliance
Ingram Content Group UK Ltd.
Pitfield, Milton Keynes, MK11 3LW, UK
UKHW040032200726
13854UKWH00001B/484

9 798201 281762